Duckula and the
Ghost Train
Mystery

This book is dedicated to you out there – *whatever* you are

Other books about Count Duckula from Carnival:

In the *Mini Hardback* series:

Vampire Vacation
Restoration Comedy
No Sax Please, We're Egyptian
The Ghost of Castle McDuckula

Duckula on Treasure Island
A novel by Joyce McAleer

The Duckula Sticker Book

JOHN BROADHEAD

Duckula and the Ghost Train Mystery

CARNIVAL

Carnival
An imprint of the Children's Division
of the Collins Publishing Group
8 Grafton Street, London W1X 3LA

Published by Carnival 1988
Reprinted 1989

Count Duckula is a registered trademark of
THAMES TELEVISION plc

ISBN 0 00 194320 8

Printed and bound in Great Britain by
Collins, Glasgow

Set in Times

1

A Stormy Night in Transylvania

Deep in the night, thunder crashed in the dark, leaden skies over Transylvania. Brilliant flashes of fork lightning lit up the jagged mountain and the wicked, hideously shaped Castle Duckula, which perched precariously on its summit.

'Oooh!' cried the cowardly, cringing peasants far below, cowering in terror behind the front doors of their disgusting hovels. 'The storm is at its height! What dastardly deeds must the dreaded Count Duckula be perpetrating up there tonight!? Will we survive this fearsome night? Will we ever eat a bowl of gruesome gruel again?'

A thousand feet above them, Count Duckula, nobleman of naughtiness and current keeper of the Castle, was indeed wide awake – and hard at work in a draughty, stone-walled room at the top of a ramshackle turret. He cackled loudly as he reached out and pulled the lever of a large electrical switch . . .

The locomotive lurched into life with a shower of sparks and started racing round the track of his model railway!

'Ah-ha!' he screamed joyfully, as he watched the little train gather speed. 'I fixed it, I fixed my engine at last!'

The little cloaked Count jumped up and started chasing round the track after his train. 'Choo, choo, chooeee! Chuff, chuff, chuff! Ta-ta ta-tum, ta-ta ta-tum. Look out, everyone, The Transylvanian Express is on its way-eee!'

At that moment his beloved Nanny had reached number 997 of the thousand or so stone steps that spiralled up to Duckula's bedroom. When she heard the Count's running footsteps and whooping noises, her beak opened in alarm. She hurried up the few remaining steps and lurched at the hefty wooden door.

'Ooh, me little Duckyboo's taken a turn for the worse! He's flipped his bloomin' lid!' Then she shouted, 'It's all right, Nanny's here – with some 'ot cocoa with chocolatey bits floatin' on top!'

'Aaargh, no – not *you*, Nanny!' screamed Duckula from the other side of the door. 'No, no, no! Let me move my train set. Be careful, Na – '

Sadly, the word *careful* wasn't in Nanny's dictionary; she'd never known the meaning of the word, and had certainly never been blessed with the quality. The way she was built didn't help either; think of a hen the size of a double-decker bus, and you have an excellent picture of Nanny.

'Be *what*?' she cried in her faltering falsetto voice, as she smashed through the oak door of the bedroom and appeared in a haze of flying splinters.

Duckula was resigned – and already on the phone. 'Scroggins, the builders? . . . that's right, it's Castle Duckula . . . new door, please . . . top room, back turret. . . . see my butler Igor when you come to fit it . . . thanks, 'bye!'

'You orderin' another new door, Duckyboos?' Nanny enquired. 'I don't know what you does with 'em!'

'*Me?* What do *I* do with them?' Duckula asked her incredulously. He tapped her forehead with a knuckle. 'Solid wood, just as I thought. Is there any point in trying to explain? I suppose you may evolve eventually. In a couple of thousand years, after a couple more millions of doors, you may just start to think momentarily; a tiny spark of an idea may develop deep in the numbness of your brain – before you smash through yet another door . . .'

'I can't think what you're on about, I really can't,' complained Nanny. 'Here's your cocoa. Time you was in bed, you young scallywag!'

'"Here's your cocoa! Time you was in bed, you young scallywag!"' Duckula mimicked Nanny's high-pitched voice. 'Honestly, Nanny, you're like a robot. You say the same ol' things day in day out.'

'What on earth's that little funnel stickin' up between me toes for?' pondered Nanny, stretching forward to observe her feet.

'See what I mean?' scoffed Duckula. He copied her again, '"What on earth's that little funnel stickin' up between me toes for?"' He stopped and gulped. 'Say, you don't usually say *that* . . .'

He glanced down, and his eyes followed Nanny's legs down to her big, flat feet. His beak quivered in

7

rage and despair as he saw the splattered remains of his model locomotive protruding from under her soles. The track, too, was flat as a pancake – even flatter than Nanny's feet – where she'd stood on it.

'Ere, what's that steam stuff comin' out of your ears, Duckyboos? You want to watch your blood pressure, y'know!'

'It's anger, Nanny . . .!' Duckula began calmly, shaking as he tried to contain his rage. 'Pure, un-adulterated ANGER!!!' Then he broke into a fit of noisy crying, fell forward onto the floor and started to beat it. 'Nanny – you're a ninny, you know that? A first-class, top-notch, premium N-I-N-N-Y!'

'Now, now, you know tantrums get you nowhere!'

'Oh, yes they do!' Duckula continued to hammer on the floor. 'They get me all sorts of things – broccoli sandwiches in the middle of the night, and chocolate lollipops for breakfast. But, in this case, they help me get my sanity back when I have to live with a birdbrain like you!'

The young Count's face had returned to its usual expression – not usual by Transylvanian standards, where a scowl is the norm – but okay for a young vampire who had grown up to be a fun-loving vegetarian, instead of one of those blood-sucking ghouls we all know and avoid.

'Just think, Nanny,' he began. 'Well, I know you can't actually *think* – you just sort of point your mind in a vague direction. But do your best to imagine what would have happened if you'd been George Stephenson's nanny. We'd all still be going around

8

in horse-and-carts – because with *you* around, he'd never have got the steam-engine off the ground!'

'Off the ground!' enthused Nanny. 'Do they 'ave flyin' trains nowadays? I wouldn't mind goin' on one o' them!'

'Do you honestly think you could ever get airborne?' Duckula retorted wickedly, still smarting over the total write-off of his railway. 'There's not enough aviation fuel on the whole of Planet Earth to do *that*!'

'Really?' Nanny looked pleased as she considered Duckula's cutting remark. 'How wonderful of you to say so.'

'That was an insult!' screamed Duckula in frustration. 'Oh boy, you're incorrigible, Nanny!'

'Well, don't you go incorrigin' me, then, me young fellow. Hey, where you goin'?'

Duckula, in desperation, was making for the window. He flung it open and screamed hysterically into the dark night air, 'He-elp, somebody save me! Somebody take me away from this bonehead of a Nanny! I never asked for Nanny! What have I done to deserve her?'

Down below, by the great oak front door, Igor the butler was humming a dreary funeral march as he placed the empty milk bottles on the doorstep. Why he bothered, he didn't really know, for milkmen rarely ever ventured to the threshold of Castle Duckula. In fact, there hadn't been a delivery for close on thirty years; the pile of empties was getting rather large!

9

'Nanny is just more than flesh and blood can stand!' came Duckula's voice through the thin night air.

Igor looked up and licked his lips. 'Flesh and blood, eh?' he murmured with relish. 'Now that's my kind of talk! Hee, hee, hee.'

He stood for a moment, looking out at the bleak Transylvanian landscape and the twinkling lights in the village at the bottom of the mountain. The rain had stopped now and a fresh east wind blew round his stooping form, making the tails of his butler's jacket flap wildly like a kite.

'Lovely chilly night,' he murmured. 'Makes one glad to be alive . . . or whatever. Pity the storm's over; I like it wet. Bit more mist around and it'd be just right.' He drew in a long breath, then choked and spluttered. 'Dear me, the air's a bit fresh for my liking. I much prefer a north wind; it's always perfumed with those lovely stale gasses from the marshland.'

He turned and walked in through the open doorway and slowly and deliberately closed the front door. It shut smoothly and silently.

'How ear-splittingly horrible!' mused Igor. 'No creaking noise whatsoever. Tomorrow I must call in a workman and have the hinges *de-oiled* . . .'

2
The End of the Line

'You see, Nanny, what I *really* want to do in life is – ' began Duckula, then he stopped and sighed as he discovered that his arms were pinned to his side. 'Nanny – one question first: why do you insist on tucking me into bed so tightly that I can't move a muscle?'

'There's no need *for* you to move,' Nanny answered. She flopped on to a stool by Duckula's bed. The legs groaned, splintered and gave way – but Nanny didn't even notice that she'd dropped down by half a metre. 'No need at all when you've got your ol' Nanny to do everythin' for you. You just lie back and go to sleep like a good duck and let me read you a bedtime story!'

'I want to explain something very profound to you, Nanny, but I find it most difficult when my arms are imprisoned by these sheets. It's humiliating for an articulate chap like me . . . I feel as if I'm under interrogation or something.'

'Get away with you! Only lorries is articulate. You can't fool your ol' Nanny with your fancy long words. Now, which story shall I tell you tonight?' Nanny stroked her beak, as if in deep thought. A strange whirring noise came from her head.

'Careful, Nanny,' scoffed Duckula, 'your brain's

working overtime. Whoops, what am I saying? I mean the space in your skull – where your brain should be – is working overtime.'

'I've got it! "Wispy Willie the Magic Goblin goes into the Fairy Ring" – we've not had that one for ages!'

'You're quite right, Nanny! Why, it must be all of two nights since I heard *that* classic! But don't you honestly think it's time we moved on a little in the world of literature? Couldn't we try a little Tolstoy for a change? A drop of Dickens? A spot of Robert Louis Stevenson?'

'Oh, 'im!' Nanny's dim eyes lit up momentarily. ''Im that invented them flyin' steam engines, you mean? 'Ere, why 'ave you started bangin' your head against the pillow?'

'It's quite simple, Nanny! In an effort to avoid having to stare into your – your unique face or listen to your endless drivel for a second longer, I'm trying to beat myself into a state of unconsciousness. But it's proving rather difficult with a soft feather pillow!'

'Silly boy!' said Nanny. She fished about in the sling on her right arm and produced a battered volume, which she opened and proceeded to read from. 'Ah, yes . . . Once upon a time, long, long ago, there was a little goblin called Wispy Willie, who lived deep in – *your cocoa*!'

'Deep in my cocoa?' Duckula blinked in surprise. 'This is a new twist to the Wispy Willie saga!'

'No, I mean your cocoa, Duckyboos – there on your table! You've not drunk it!'

'You're right, Nanny!' Duckula replied, seeing a

chance to escape from his mummy's tomb of a bed. 'But how can I drink when I'm all tucked up?'

'There's only one thing to be done, then!' Nanny pulled away the tight blankets and freed the young Count. Drink up an' keep your insides wet.'

'About time too!' said Duckula indignantly, picking up his cup of cocoa and sipping at it. 'Mmmm! You may be a complete duffer, but one thing you *can* do is make cocoa. Correction – the *only* thing you can do is make cocoa.'

'There's a lovely little snack for you,' beamed Nanny lovingly, as she picked up a plate containing an enormous broccoli sandwich from the bedside table and placed it on Duckula's knees. 'But you must promise you'll go to the bathroom and brush your beak before you goes to sleep. Now, when you're ready, we'll get on with your story.'

Nanny looked away for a moment to adjust the sling which supported her arm. Duckula saw his chance! He lifted up the top slice of bread, inserted the dreaded story-book into the sandwich, and then replaced the slice.

'Nice to be comfortable!' Nanny shrugged her shoulder repeatedly until her sling felt right. She turned back to Duckula. 'Now where's me Wispy Willie book? I'm sure it was 'ere on the duvet.'

'Never mind, Ninny – I mean Nanny,' said Duckula, faking concern. 'It'll turn up sometime.'

'Oh, I likes to know exactly where things are! A place for everythin' an' everythin' in its – er – er – '

'Broccoli sandwich?' teased Duckula.

13

'Thats it – everythin' in its broccoli sandwich! 'Ang on, talkin' about broccoli sandwiches, I see you've not touched yours . . .'

'Not hungry at the moment, Nanny. I'll eat it later.'

'Not 'ungry? Not H-U-N-G-R-Y? I've never 'eard you say that before. You must be under the weather. Come on, eat it up – it'll do you the world of good!'

'No, Nanny, no, no, NO!' Duckula's eyes bulged out like ping-pong balls as Nanny playfully prised his beak open, pushed the sandwich into his mouth and held it close until he agreed to chew. It was no use arguing with Nanny; she didn't know her own strength. Even at play she had the power and nimbleness of a giant excavator.

'There we are – down the 'atch. We 'as to keep up our strength if we're goin' to be Master of the Castle, don't we?'

'Gloop, gloop, glob!' gurgled Duckula, as the last remaining traces of bread, broccoli and Wispy Willie the Magic Goblin disappeared forever down his throat. 'I'm not *going to be* Master of the Castle, Nanny – I already *am*! So how come you treat me like a kid?'

'Oooh, you'll always be Nanny's little Duckyboos. Come 'ere an' let me give you a big squeeze an' a cuddle.'

'HELPPPPP!' screamed Duckula. 'Last time you did that you cracked all my ribs! Save me, someone, SAVE ME!'

Nanny's attention was diverted by a sudden click

of the latch on the bedroom door. Slowly the door started to creak open. Nanny and Duckula stood transfixed as a horrible handful of bunched fingers appeared at the edge of the door.

'Wh-what is it? A bloomin' monster or somethin'?' wailed Nanny.

The door opened further. Nanny fell clumsily to the floor and scrambled to hide under Duckula's bed. It was a hopeless attempt, for the bottom half of her body stuck out like an inflated hippopotamus in a pinafore.

'Wh-who's there?' inquired the nervous occupant of the bed, which was now a couple of metres in the air, balancing precariously across Nanny's back.

A huge, greenish-yellow beak came round the door, followed by a wrinkled, drooping face with sad, despairing eyes: the sort of face, reader, you could have encountered only in your most fiendishly horrible nightmares.

'Oh, it's *you*, Igor!' Duckula panted in relief, wiping a bead – in truth, more like a sinkful – of sweat from his brow. 'Why are you creeping around like that? This castle is spooky enough as it is!'

'I do apologize most humbly, Master Duckula, Sir . . . but I didn't want to disturb you if you were asleep.'

'Me – asleep? Fat chance of that with this walking marquee around!' Duckula pointed below to Nanny. 'What did you come up for, anyway?'

'To collect your cocoa cup, if I may, Sir.' Igor stepped forward hesitantly. A loud metallic crunching noise came from beneath his feet. He stopped and peered down. 'Oh, dear me, milord!'

'You may have come to collect my cocoa cup, Igor, old pal,' said Duckula wistfully, 'but it looks to me as if you've also come to complete the destruction of my model railway! You've just finished off the rest of the rolling-stock – the dining-car and the first-class no-smoking compartment!'

3
Duckula's Big Idea

'As I started to say last night,' began Duckula the following morning at the breakfast table, 'what I really want to be in life is a – '

''Ere, shall I shake up your ketchup, Duckyboos?' inquired Nanny dutifully. Without waiting for an answer, she put down her copy of the Transylvanian times, leapt clumsily from her chair at the long dining-table and raced to Duckula, who was perched at the opposite end.

'Oh, for goodness' sake, Nanny, why can't you ever listen to what I have to say?'

Nanny ignored him and furrowed her brow in concentration as she snatched up the bottle of sauce by his side and began shaking it violently.

Duckula watched spellbound; he knew what was going to happen! The bottle slipped out of her grasp, clean across the room, right through a pane of window-glass and down the steep mountainside.

Duckula glanced at the second-finger of his wristwatch. 'Five . . . four . . . three . . . two . . . one!'

'Ye-owwww!' came a pathetic, far-off scream, precisely on cue, as an ungrateful peasant down in the village below received an unexpected bump on the head.

'Congratulations, Nanny, you're improving!' said

Duckula sarcastically, taking up half a loaf of bread and buttering it greedily. 'At least broken windows are cheaper to replace than smashed doors!'

Nanny stared guiltily towards the smashed glass.

'Cat got your tongue?' asked Duckula, spooning half a jar of strawberry jam on to his gigantic sandwich. 'No fear of that. It'd take a lion to get *your* tongue, Nanny, and then it would have to be specially trained to overcome the fear of putting its head in your beak. Hey, *trained*! That reminds me of what I keep trying to tell you: I have decided to be – sure you don't want to interrupt, Nanny? Okay, here goes – I have decided to become an engine driver! There, I said it, I said IT!'

Nanny turned to Duckula. Her beak began to open.

Duckula was delighted. 'Boy, this is my lucky day! Looks like I'm about to get an intelligent response – well, a response, at least.'

Nanny's beak opened wider. She pointed a finger in mid-air, as if she were about to issue an important statement. 'I think,' she began. 'I think – '

'Yes, yes?' Duckula urged her. 'Good idea for me to become an engine driver?'

'I think . . . I've got more sauce in the larder!'

In exasperation Duckula picked up a large silver tea-tray and polished it with his elbow until it shone like a mirror. 'Nanny, if you don't listen to me, I'll confront you with the ultimate threat! I'll make you look at something absolutely disgustingly obnoxious – the reflection of your own face in this tray!'

'You know what?' Nanny bumbled on, not listening to Duckula, as she poured him a glass of lemonade. 'You should be an *engine-driver*!'

Duckula gulped and dropped the tray in surprise. 'Did you say an engine-driver, Nanny?'

'That's what I said,' confirmed Nanny. 'I was thinkin' last night, after I trod on your toy train, it's just the life for a young duck. Get you out of this gloomy castle a bit more . . . put some colour in your cheeks!'

'Am I hearing things?' Duckula pinched his cheek. 'Ouch! I'm not dreaming either!'

'An' this mornin' I spotted an advert for a real steam locomotive in me paper when I was readin' me horror scope.'

'Horoscope, you mean, Nanny; although, in your case, maybe horror scope is more accurate. Did it say you were going to make cocoa and drive me bats for the next eight or nine hundred years? Hee, hee!'

'Eh?'

'Never mind, Nanny. It was just a joke. I can't wait for it to sink in. Go on, tell me about this loco!'

'I'll do better than that, Duckyboos, I'll show you the advert.' She waddled across to the other end of the table, picked up The Transylvanian Times and returned to Duckula.

'Now, let's 'ave a look.' She thumbed through the pages. 'Hearses For Hire . . . Haunted Holiday Homes . . . Monster Spares . . . Racks, Pillories and Guillotines . . . Ah, 'ere it is!'

Duckula snatched the paper and followed Nanny's finger to a little display advertisement:

For Sale

ONE STEAM LOCOMOTIVE

In Good Clanking Order

Only £20

Apply to
Mr Horace Trumpetblower
Hard Cheese Hotel
Pendingle
Cornwall
ENGLAND

'Gee, Nanny! It's like a dream come true – and what a snip at only £20. I'd better be quick or it'll be gone!' Duckula jumped up and down in joy and quite forgot about his breakfast. 'What's the phone number? Aw, there isn't one; I'll have to go round in person!'

The kitchen door opened and Igor bumbled in silently with a fresh pot of tea.

'Good mornin', Mr Igor!' squawked Nanny.

'I'd hardly go as far as to say that, Nanny. Perfectly dreadful, actually.'

'The young Master's goin' to buy a real steam engine today!' continued Nanny with uncharacteristic enthusiasm.

'Really? How – ambitious of him,' murmured Igor, placing the teapot firmly on the table in front of Duckula. 'Pardon me for sounding a little negative, Sir, but I suspect that the Trans-Transylvanian Express Railway Company won't take too kindly to joyriders scooting up and down their line in a pirate locomotive. Has milord considered precisely where he's going to run it?'

Duckula hadn't, of course. 'You've got a good point there, Igor.' He drummed his fingers on the table and sucked his thumb whilst he thought deeply for two seconds. 'But I have a plan!'

'I never doubted it for a moment,' sighed Igor in his deep, rumbling voice. 'And I was hoping for a quiet day . . .'

'I think I'll run it,' Duckula's mind was working at full steam now, 'I think I'll run it – round and round the mountain up to the Castle. That's it – a spiral track from the bottom to the top.'

'Oooh, that would be 'andy for the shops, Duckyboos!' cried Nanny. 'Jus' the bloomin' job!'

'It would make us accessible to the world!' enthused Duckula. 'The peasants from the village could come up and see the Castle on a Sunday afternoon. Hey, we could turn the grounds into a theme park!'

'Oh, dear, this is *not* a pleasant idea!' grumbled

21

Igor to himself. Then he spoke out loud, 'Begging your pardon, milord, but I hardly think – '

'Correct!' interrupted Duckula impudently. 'You hardly think! Nanny hardly thinks! It's me who has to do all the thinking round here. Goodness knows what would happen to the place if I weren't around.'

'Ouch!' grimaced Igor. 'I wish you wouldn't persist in using that awful word, Sir!'

'What? *Goodness*, you mean, Igor?' taunted Duckula. 'Goodness me, fancy not liking a good word like – um – goodness. Goodness gracious me!'

Igor, cringing and wincing, sat on a dining-chair and mopped his brow with his handkerchief.

'You'll love Duckula World, Igor. We can have roundabouts, and candy-floss stalls . . .'

'No, please, no . . .!'

'And guided tours of the Castle . . .'

'How agonizing . . .'

'And little old me will be driving my engine all day long – bringing hundreds of jolly peasants to spend their drachmas – and then taking them back to the village at the end of the day!'

Igor's hooded eyes opened a little, as he savoured a gruesome thought. 'Wait a moment – hundreds of peasants, eh? That means I could probably nab a few for my dungeon without anyone noticing . . .'

'No chance,' scoffed Duckula. 'You'll be too busy – inspecting my passengers' tickets!'

'An' I can make cocoa!' chipped in Nanny.

'No you can't, Nanny. You can *nearly* make cocoa – but not quite!'

Nanny was puzzling over this comment, as Duck-ula picked up a large shopping-bag and raced to the refrigerator. He swung open the door and started scooping armfuls of food into the bag.

'What you doin' with all that, Duckyboos?' inquired Nanny.

'Supplies, Nanny, for the journey to England. It's a long way off, y'know.'

'Beats me why we don't just travel in the Castle. Be a lot bloomin' quicker!'

Duckula stopped in mid-cheese. 'Of course! The Castle will take us there in a trice. Why didn't I think of that? Why did *you* think of it? In fact, *how* did you think of it?' He dropped the food on the floor, snatched up Nanny's newspaper and ran to the kitchen-door.

'Come on, Igor! Bring some English money! Chop, chop, Nanny! To the cellar . . .'

4
The Castle Moves!

Duckula hurried down the well-worn steps two at a
time to the dank, dark dungeons, closely followed –
well, not that closely – by Nanny and Igor.

'Brrr! This part of the Castle really gives me the
creeps!' he shivered, stepping gingerly into the
stately upright coffin that rested there in the grim,
desperate surroundings.

New readers – you naughty creatures, you really
should bone up on Duckula folklore! – must understand that this terrifying tomb is the operational
nerve-centre of a magical travelling mechanism. It
can take the Castle anywhere in the world – and
probably the universe too – in the eyelid of a bat.
Sorry, the bat of an eyelid!

Exactly how it works, and precisely what physical
actions our feathered friend carries out in his terrifying tomb, may not be revealed on these pages. It
is a secret known only to members of the dreaded
Duckula line. Anyway, who really cares? Quite
frankly, I gather that Duckula is not too familiar
with the secret himself, if his geographical aim is
anything to go by. You'll see what I mean by reading
on . . .

'Mmmm!' came Duckula's voice from inside the
coffin. 'Now where *is* Pendingle, when it's at home?

Nope, can't spot it on the map; can't even see Cornwall actually . . . Ah, there's London; we'll go there and walk the rest of the way . . .'

With a horrifying hum and a terrific trembling, Duckula's coffin began to shake. Then the whole Castle began to shake. Then Nanny's knees began to shake.

'Better sit on the floor, Mr Igor,' she suggested. 'Looks like we're in for a rough ride!'

'Unfortunately life has always been a rough ride for me, Nanny,' mused Igor philosophically, his legs creaking as he joined Nanny on the floor. 'If only I'd been born into money and had a place of my own . . . a nasty little cottage, overgrown with waist-high weeds, set in a secluded, dark, haunted, forest.'

''Ang on!' cried Nanny, not listening to the rambling butler, 'We're off!'

Down in the village the peasants ran into their smelly little houses and hid behind their front doors, as the whole mountain began to vibrate. Coloured flashes of light radiated from the high-up Castle, and the hum grew deafeningly loud until it became unbearable. Then, with a shattering thunderclap noise, the Castle was gone, and the mountain and village were left to enjoy a strange, silent stillness.

'Eh, what a relief! Them up at Castle 'ave gone out fer the day,' mumbled Ludmilla, an unwashed peasant washerwoman, running wretchedly out into the village high street – a cart-track of soggy mud.

'Good riddance, I say!' answered her revolting husband, who was so horridly poor that he didn't

25

even have a name. 'But the Castle will be back all right. Come the dawn, it'll be back!'

So it was, so it is – and so it always will be. Castle Duckula always returns to the mountain automatically at dawn, Eastern Transylvanian time. You knew that, didn't you, readers? Well, you should have done!

Crunch! Splat! The Castle landed with a jolt. Duckula emerged dizzily from the coffin. 'Handbrake on, into neutral!' he joked to Nanny and Igor, who had rolled into a corner and were lying in a tangled heap of beaks and legs.

''Ere, get out of me sling, Mr Igor!' exclaimed Nanny.

'I haven't the slightest intention of lingering in your sling for a second longer than is humanly – or should I say creaturely – possible,' complained Igor, struggling to remove one of his bony legs from one of Nanny's bottomless pinafore pockets.

'When you have quite finished,' cackled Duckula impatiently, starting up the stairs, 'you can join me at the front door and we'll set out for Pendingle.'

Meanwhile the two bats in the Castle Clock were recovering from being catapulted out upon impact.

'Boy!' said Dmitri. 'I think I just bust a spring. You know what this Castle needs, Sviatoslav? Shock absorbers!'

'Shock absorbers, you say?' answered Sviatoslav. 'You couldn't get shock absorbers that would cope with all the shocks you get in *this* place. There are shocks round every corner – the butler, Nanny, the duck with the cloak . . .!'

The bats collapsed with laughter.

'Hee, hee, hee!' choked Dmitri. 'A good one, Sviatoslav. I never laughed like that since – since – '

'Since my last joke!' screamed his friend, now in hysterics.

Then they fell about giggling again.

At the front door stood Duckula, Igor and Nanny. Duckula had called in at the kitchen *en route* and refilled his shopping bag with food.

'Allow me, Sir, to open the door,' said Igor dutifully.

'Why, thank you, Igor. Very nice of you,' said Duckula.

'It's not very nice of him at all!' shrilled Nanny in her high-pitched voice. 'It's 'is job. He don't want to become repugnant!'

'*Redundant*, Nanny, is the word I think you're after,' chortled Duckula. 'He already *is* repugnant!'

'Very *droll*, milord, I must say!' Igor looked a little hurt. He considered himself to be rather on the handsome side.

Nanny was about to open her beak to ask what *droll* meant, when Igor dragged open the huge door and let in a gust of cool air. 'Oooh, it's proper chilly!' she said instead.

A peculiar sight met the travellers' eyes. All they could see stretching before them were row upon row of high green hedges, some at right-angles to the other.

'Crumbs!' cried Duckula. 'This doesn't look like merry old England to me. Where are all the red London buses? And the black taxis? And all the people?'

Igor scratched the side of his beak thoughtfully. 'If I might hazard a guess, Sir, I would say you've landed the Castle bang in the centre of Hampton Court Maze!'

'A maze! I've never been in a maze before! What fun!' Duckula skipped outside. 'I love a challenge, don't you, Nanny?'

Nanny looked blank. 'Oo-er, I don't think I've ever had one of them!'

Igor buttoned his jacket and pulled up his collar. The fresh air wasn't to his liking: he'd been hoping for a damp, muggy atmosphere with a touch of London fog, if at all possible.

'I'll look after your snacks, Duckyboos,' announced Nanny, picking up Duckula's bulging shopping bag and dropping it effortlessly into her sling. It seemed to disappear without trace.

For almost an hour Duckula raced backwards and forwards around the maze, with Nanny and Igor trailing loyally behind him. Eventually he came, panting, to a standstill.

'Let's get the provisions out, Nanny,' he said. 'I'm famished!'

'Get the what out, Duckyboos?'

'The food, Nanny! Fuh-oooh-duh, FOOD!'

Nanny obeyed – and not only did she bring out the food from her sling, but also a big china pot of piping hot tea.

'Beats me how you do that!' said Duckula, intrigued as ever by Nanny's ability to produce virtually anything from a first-class stamp to a grand piano at a moment's notice.

He chomped greedily into a fresh broccoli sandwich. 'Why don't you join me in a sandwich, Nanny?' Realizing what he'd said, and knowing Nanny's reputation for taking things literally, he hastily rephrased the question. 'I mean, *do* take a sandwich! You, too, Igor.'

Igor declined the offer; any food with less than 100% meat content was of no interest to him. Nanny, however, was a different kettle of fish: she devoured the plate of sandwiches in a couple of quick gobbles.

'Excuse me,' came a polite, slightly hoarse voice from behind Duckula, 'but would there be any chance of sharing a spot of your food?'

'There would have been if you'd beaten Nanny to the plate!' quipped Duckula. 'Hey, who *is* that?'

He whipped round to find a short, tubby fellow wearing a smart overcoat and a bowler hat.

'Wotsit,' said the stranger. 'Dr Wotsit.'

'Oooh, a *doctor*!' exclaimed Nanny, displaying an obvious adoration for the medical profession. 'You can look at the corns on me feet an' give me some fresh ointment!'

'Not before he eats, Nanny – and preferably not

29

at all.' Duckula rummaged through his shopping bag and brought out a murky green-yellow apple, which he handed to the doctor.

'Funny colour,' murmured Dr Wotsit, eyeing the apple curiously with some suspicion.

'Take it or leave it, Doc; there's nothing else,' said Duckula cockily. 'All the apples grow that yucky colour where we come from!'

Wotsit sniffed the apple, shrugged his shoulders and sunk his teeth into the grotesque piece of fruit. 'Mmmm, not bad, not bad at – *good heavens!*'

Duckula thought the good doctor had maybe hit a maggot, but then he realized that he was expressing concern at the Castle. 'Oh, the old gothic monstrosity? That's where we live. The other two old gothic monstrosities you see here are Nanny and Igor, my two – er – companions. I'm Duckula, by the way.'

Wotsit nodded to Igor and Nanny and then continued to stare in wonder at the Castle.

'Not much – but we call it home,' said Duckula genially. 'Take a look around, if you like; the key's under the mat. But please excuse me – we gotta get out of the Maze.'

'I can help you there,' said Wotsit quickly. 'By using the scientific and logical science of deductive reasoning, taught to me by close friend, mentor and colleague, Mr Hemlock Jones, the best and most famous detective in all of – '

'Can we cut the speech?' urged Duckula. 'If you can show us out – please *do* it!'

4

On the Way to Cornwall

One hour later – and Duckula, Nanny and Igor were still deep in Hampton Court Maze.

'Coo-eee!' came Dr Wotsit's voice from a distance. 'You still there, Mr Duckula?'

'Of course we are!' yelled Duckula irritably. He lowered his voice to speak to Nanny and Igor. 'Not only has he led us on a wild goose chase, he's also succeeded in separating himself from us! So much for his powers of deduction and logic!'

'I'm afraid I'm back in the centre . . . by your magnificent castle!' shouted Wotsit.

'Well, go and – oh, go and have some biscuits and milk in the kitchen!' cried Duckula. 'We'll manage by ourselves, thank you very much!'

'Any jammy ones?'

'Oh, boy! Do *I* meet 'em!' fumed Duckula.

'Top shelf over the sink, in the tin with fairies on it!' screeched Nanny to Wotsit.

'Well, thank you, too, Nanny!' Duckula waved a threatening finger at her. 'Giving away my favourites now!'

Nanny looked sheepish and tried to change the subject. She glanced all around. 'If only there was a door, Duckyboos . . .'

'Oh, yes! Super maze that'd be, with doors in it; a

real test of skill that would make . . .' Duckula stopped babbling. 'Hey, that's the answer! Doors! Of course! Nanny, pretend there's a door right here in the hedge, and then in every hedge beyond it. Now, show me how you'd go through them all . . .'

Bam! Bam! Bam! Bam! Nanny marched resolutely on, smashing effortlessly through each hedge she came to, leaving a huge gaping hole, through which Duckula and Igor followed.

The three travellers reached the outside of the Maze, but Nanny, upon demolishing the final hedge had knocked over and trampled into the ground a small crow-like attendant wearing a mean little moustache and a peaked cap.

'Oi!' groaned the attendant. 'What's the meanin' of wreckin' the Maze? Hedges don't grow on trees, y'know.'

Nanny, concerned, helped the attendant to his feet and dusted him down by slapping him on the back with hefty strokes. But she simply winded him with each stroke.

'Will – *uh* – you – *uh* – kindly stop that, madam? Thank you. Now, do you realize you 'ave all committed a very serious offence?' He eyed Duckula, Nanny and Igor carefully and then continued, 'You *are* a funny-looking bunch! Are you sleeping rough?'

Igor was incensed by this last remark. 'Indeed we are not! You are, my man, in the noble presence of Count Duckula of Transylvania, and Nanny and I are his servants!'

'Stone me – aristocrats!' chuckled the attendant

sarcastically. 'Smart cloak, Mr – er – Count Jugular, was it?'

'Duck-u-lah!' said Duckula. 'I'm sorry about the hedge. I'll pay for the damage – '

'Oh, that's all right, Count,' smirked the attendant. 'You jet-setters, you like your moments of fun – even if it means I've got to spend a fortnight or so on me poor knees, plantin' new 'edges an' then waitin' for 'em to grow. In ten or fifteen years the Maze'll be as good as new – if I live to see it, that is . . .'

'Oh, what a tale of woe . . . I apologize, I apologize!' cried Duckula. He whispered to Igor, 'Give him a tip and let's get on our way!'

Igor fumbled in his pocket and handed a small coin to the attendant, who then fell to his knees, clutching the money. 'A fortune . . . a king's ransome . . . it's far too much for me. What shall I buy first? An expensive Italian sports-car? A yacht?'

'A book of acting lessons!' commented Duckula. 'I've never seen such an over-the-top performance! Are you for real?'

The attendant paused for a moment and then suddenly dashed his cap to the ground. 'No I'm not for real!' He wriggled out of his jacket, ripped off his moustache, pulled out a deerstalker hat from inside his shirt and placed it on his head. 'Congratulations on your observation! You guessed who I am!'

'Er – who *are* you?' asked Duckula, dumbfounded.

33

'You don't *know* me? You don't recognize the world's greatest living detective?'

'Oh, you must be Shylock Bones – er – Eyebrow Combs – '

'Hemlock Jones!' exclaimed the ex-Maze attendant, holding out a business-card. 'At your service!'

'And you're looking for your friend and colleague, Dr Wotsit?'

'Why, yes! Brilliant observation, my dear friend. A capital piece of work. However did you – '

'The Doc's stuck in the Maze; you'd better get him out,' said Duckula, itching to get away. 'Before you go, can you put us in the direction of Cornwall?'

'Cornwall . . . Cornwall . . .' Jones looked defeated, then he pointed vaguely due west. 'That way, my dear fellow. Charming location.'

'Far?'

'Well, all distances are relative, aren't they? I mean, compared with the distance between Earth and the Sun, it's nothing is it? I'd say about three hundred-ish miles! Toodle-pip for now!'

He disappeared into the Maze, leaving the Transylvanian trio in a state of agitation.

'Three hundred miles!' echoed Duckula. 'And I thought England was a titchy place. You don't have a helicopter in your sling by any chance, Nanny?'

''Fraid not, Duckyboos. If you were to ask me for a jar of pickles or a crêpe bandage, I might be able to say *yes*. Or maybe – '

'Yes, I get the picture, Nanny. Anything, basically, of no possible use to anyone.'

34

Igor coughed. 'This air's uncommonly fresh for London, milord. Why don't we make for the city-centre? I believe they have some delicious fogs; thick traffic fumes at the very least!'

'This isn't a sight-seeing tour, Igor!' Duckula reminded his butler. 'We're on an assignment, remember? It's Cornwall we want – not Hadrian's Wall!'

''Adrian's Wall is nowhere near London!' piped Nanny. 'It's way up north, stretching from the Solway Firth right across to the mouth of the Tyne. Built in the second century, it was.'

'I suppose you were there at the time,' said Duckula, hardly listening. 'They probably used you as scaffolding.'

'No, what we want,' Nanny continued, 'is to get a bus to Paddington Station, then take the 3.15 train to Penzance. Oooh, a *train* – me little dumplin'! P'raps the driver will let you work the controls!'

It dawned on Duckula that Nanny was talking sense for the first time in her life. 'Hey, how come you know about Hadrian's Wall all of a sudden – *and* how to get to Cornwall?'

'Easy! It's 'ere in this little book I found in me sling: *The Transylvanian Travellers' Guide to Great Britain*. Don't know where Great Britain is; must be somewhere round 'ere, I reckon!'

'Nanny – you're *not* a ninny!' Duckula took her and Igor by the hand. 'Come on, quickly! I can see a bus in the distance!'

To cut a long story short – and, let's face it, *any*

story about Duckula is best cut short! – the young Count, Nanny and Igor eventually found themselves hurtling along on the 3.15 train, bound for their Cornish destination.

It had been a tedious trip across London, to say the least. Nanny had been refused entry, first on to a London bus, and then into a taxi; quite reasonably because in both cases she simply wouldn't fit through the door. The Underground had proved slightly more accommodating, but here Igor had turned out to be the drawback, because his feet were too un-coordinated to step onto the moving staircases. Nanny had solved the problem by picking him up and carrying him down, protesting, like an enormous, overgrown babe-in-arms.

But now they were on their way! Duckula sat reading a comic, and Igor, next to him, was fast asleep and snoring heavily.

Duckula put down his comic and gazed at the lush, green, sunlit countryside racing past the window. 'Boy!' he murmured. 'Wait till I'm driving my *own* engine!'

He lurched about in his seat, pulling all kinds of imaginary levers and pretending to shovel coal into the fiery boiler. 'Wheeeeee!' he whistled. 'Off the line, you village peasants! Make way for the Duckula Express!'

Igor awoke with a start. 'Peasants? Where?! I'm hungry! Open the dungeons . . .!' He came quickly to his senses and then screwed up his eyes. 'Drat, the sun's come out. How uncomfortable. May I borrow your publication, milord, to cover my eyes?'

Duckula slapped his comic into Igor's lap. 'Fine company you make, Igor – you might as well be dead.'

'Promises, promises!' sighed Igor deeply, closing his eyes, leaning back and placing the comic over his face. 'Ah, that's much more like it . . . beautiful, beautiful darkness!'

Duckula pulled a rude face at Igor, then stood up and looked down the train. 'Where can Nanny be? It's half an hour since I packed her off to the dining-car for a salad sandwich. You just *can't* seem to get the staff nowadays!'

5

The Pendingle Connection

Nanny was being chatted up. In the dining-car she'd struck up a conversation with a lively Italian waiter, who was serving snacks and drinks.

'You're-a from-a Transylvania? How wonderful! I've-a been there for my holidays,' chirped the small, suntanned cuckoo-like fellow. He twisted the ends of his long drooping moustache and rolled his eyes. 'Zee girls, they are all-a so pretty – like *you*, Senorina!'

'Oh, get away with you!' squawked Nanny, flattered by his attentions. She blushed and attempted to give him a friendly nudge but, in her nervous embarrassment, she pushed a little too hard and knocked him to the floor. Sandwiches and pork pies flew everywhere.

'And you're *so* demonstrative!' purred the waiter from under his counter.

By the time Duckula, now starving hungry, reached the dining-car, Nanny was deep in conversation with her admirer, and on first-name terms. 'Oh, yes, Toni, I watch a lot of television back at 'ome. I like the cartoons best – they 'as me in stitches!'

She turned to greet Duckula. 'Hello, Duckyboos. This is Toni. 'E knows Transylvania. 'E's been there for 'is 'olidays.'

'Is he nuts?' joked Duckula.

'And this 'ere is me little Duckyboos, Toni,' went on Nanny. ''E's a count.'

'A count?' smiled Toni. 'You mean one, two, three?'

'Oooh, I'm not sayin' he can count that far – not yet, anyway!' said Nanny, following up the comment with a shrill and prolonged whooping laugh.

'Ho, ho, ho! Hee, hee!' Toni threw back his head and joined her in peals of laughter.

'Tut! They're worse than the peasants!' Duckula's eyes were drawn to a salad sandwich and a cup of coffee on the counter by Nanny's elbow. He picked them up eagerly, but found that the coffee was icy. 'Aw, Nanny, you've let my drink go stone cold. It's not even lukewarm . . .'

'It *look warm* to me, all right!' Toni exploded into another fit of giggling.

'Huh! There's no way I'm going to get any sense out of you two,' grunted Duckula. 'I'm going back to my seat!'

The train chugged on for a number of hours and arrived at Penzance in the early evening.

'Wakey, wakey, Duckyboos. I think we're 'ere!'

Duckula opened his eyes and found Nanny sitting in the seat opposite. 'Nice to have you back with us, Nanny!'

'I've been back ages,' said Nanny. 'You've been asleep for a long time, young duck. It'll do you good – fresh air an' lots of rest, that's what'll make you grow!' She stretched forward and gave him a motherly pinch on his cheek.

Duckula pulled away and glanced round self-consciously. 'I wish you wouldn't do that when people can see.'

Igor was still in dreamland. On second thoughts, he was more likely to be in nightmareland! The comic covering his face rose and fell with each breath.

Duckula removed the comic and knocked on his beak. 'Anyone at home? Come on, Igor. Time to go walkies.'

''E's sleepin' like a baby,' said Nanny. 'It's a pity to wake 'im.'

'No, it's not – it's good fun!' said Duckula impishly, now tapping insistently on Igor's beak. He called loudly to his butler, 'Rare T-bone steaks . . . roast peasants . . . torture chambers . . . giblets . . . werewolf-on-toast!'

Igor licked his beak. His eyes sprang open and he looked around greedily.

'Sorry to disappoint you, Igor,' laughed Duckula, 'but it never fails, does it? Hurry up, it's *all change* for Pendingle!'

The Transylvanian terrors left the railway-carriage and walked along the platform. As they passed the dining-car, they saw Toni the waiter through the window. He smiled adoringly at Nanny and blew a kiss to her.

'Oooh, 'e's a proper gentleman!' she shrieked. ''E

gave me 'is phone number. Says 'e'll call an' see me at the Castle nex' time 'e's in Transylvania!'

Bad news greeted the travellers at the end of the platform.

'There be no connection to Pendingle any more,' the ticket-inspector told them. 'The line's been closed for nigh on twenty years. No buses, neither, not at this time. You'll have to go by taxi, or walk it.'

Duckula didn't trouble to explain that buses and taxis were of no earthly use to any travelling party which included a member of Nanny's stature; he merely asked which way Pendingle lay.

'That be easy,' said the ticket-collector, pointing to an old rusty branch line. 'Follow the old track and it'll take you all the way. It be only 'bout ten miles.'

'Only ten? Is that all?' said Duckula sarcastically.

Dusk was falling as they plodded wearily along the edge of the narrow country road that led to the little seaside village of Pendingle. Duckula, walking in front of the others, kept a keen eye on the old railway track to make sure he didn't lose sight of it.

He glanced around and saw that Nanny had stopped to pick daisies. 'Oh, Nanny, put a spurt on. We won't be there till dawn tomorrow at this rate!'

'*Dawn* . . . that reminds me, milord,' announced Igor in a matter-of-fact voice. 'You do realize, I suppose, that the Castle will be leaving Hampton Court and returning home by itself at dawn, Eastern Transylvanian Time? And that we won't be back in time to go with it . . .'

Duckula gulped; he'd forgotten all about the Castle. 'Of course I realize it,' he answered calmly, desperately thinking of an explanation to defeat old smartypants Igor. 'It's all – um – part of the plan!'

'Plan, Sir?'

'Yes, Igor – the plan! The Castle flies back home itself, while we snap up the engine in Pendingle and drive it back to Transylvania. Now, what could be simpler than that?'

'Well, provided that no-one else has already bought your locomotive, milord, and provided that it's working, and provided that it comes with enough track to reach home, we have only to contend with the problem of getting it across the sea. We *are* on an island, you know, with respect.'

These were problems that hadn't even entered Duckula's head, but he was determined not to let Igor get the better of him. 'Why don't you ever look on the bright side, Igor? All the great innovators did. Alexander Graham Bell would never have invented the – er – doorbell if he hadn't looked on the bright side. And do you think Guglielmo Marconi would ever have discovered – um – discovered ice-cream if he hadn't kept his spirits up?'

'No, Duckyboos, you've got it all wrong! Bell invented the *telephone*, and Marconi the *radio*,' Nanny broke in. She waved a large book, *Lives of the Great Inventors,* which she'd produced from her sling.

'Nanny . . .' said Duckula.

'Yes?'

42

'Shut – your – beak!'

After five miles they were all too exhausted to walk another step, so they sat down to rest on a large fallen tree. In normal circumstances it would have been a pleasant evening for a stroll: the night air was mild, and the full moon in the cloudless sky gave enough light to see by.

'Boy, my feet are throbbing!' whined Duckula.

'I'm all in generally,' complained Igor.

'Funny – you usually come to life after dark, Mr Igor,' said Nanny.

'But I don't *usually* partake in a ten-mile hike, Nanny,' replied Igor. 'And this Cornwall place – it just doesn't give me the creeps like home does.'

Their conversation was interrupted by a low clanking noise nearby, followed by a metallic squeal of brakes and a loud hissing.

Duckula recognized it at once. 'Ah, Nanny, there's nothing like the sound of a steam-engine . . . it's pure magic! Hey, what am I saying? *Steam-engine* – here in the middle of nowhere?'

He looked across to the old railway line they were following, and there in the gloom stood a magnificent old locomotive coupled to a string of equally old-fashioned open-top carriages! The engine, gurgling and squirting beautiful white steam from its pistons, seemed alive, like a huge, friendly beast of immense strength.

Duckula was overcome by the sight and was rooted to the spot, but Igor remained practical. 'It's

43

pointing towards Pendingle, milord. I suggest we catch it.'

'Yes,' added Nanny, taking Duckula by the hand and pulling him forward. 'That blinkin' ticket-man said there were no trains to Pendingle. 'E's made us walk all this way for nothin'!'

They reached the back carriage. Igor opened the little door, climbed up and sat on one of the quaint wooden seats. Nanny, too wide for the door, found it easier to clamber straight over the side, destroying the quaint wooden seats as she did so. 'Oooh, this is smashin'!' she giggled.

None of the carriages had roofs, and Duckula could see that there were no other passengers on the train. 'Perhaps I should go and pay the driver,' he suggested. 'Can you lend me some money, Igor?'

But as Igor began the long process of searching his pockets for his wallet, the train jerked violently.

'We're going, Duckyboos!' cried Nanny. She stretched out an arm, grabbed Duckula by his cloak, pulled him inelegantly aboard and dropped him on the seat by her side.

The old train moved off slowly and then gathered speed.

'Wait!' came a strangled cry from far behind.

Duckula, Nanny and Igor turned quickly. In the half-light they could see a small, shadowy, distant figure running towards them from the road. But the train was going too fast now, and the mysterious figure soon disappeared from sight.

'How weird!' said Duckula. 'Where did *he* come from? We never saw any sign of him on the road!'

6
A Strange Occurence

The train chuffed along, its engine billowing clouds of dense steam from its tall chimney. Sparks and blobs of soot flew into the faces of the travellers, and the air was filled with the smell of red-hot coal fire.

Duckula was intoxicated by the experience. 'Nanny, do you think – do you think I *dare* hope that this is the train I'm going to buy?'

'I 'opes so, if it makes you 'appy,' squawked Nanny loudly, to overcome the sound of the clattering wheels of the carriages. 'It certainly seems a good twenty pounds worth!'

'I just hope, milord,' said Igor in a resigned voice, 'that my duties will not be extended to steaming up the boiler every morning.'

'Oh, phooey, Igor – you'll enjoy it! It's *fun*, not work!'

'Humph!' Igor was disgruntled at this remark and mumbled to himself. 'Been with the Duckulas for hundreds of years and never had to suffer like this before. Tut! A young whippersnapper of a vegetarian in charge of the Castle! If I were a few centuries younger, I'd walk out on him tomorrow and find a much more congenial position . . .'

'Beak *down*, Nanny!' yelled Duckula. 'There's a tunnel ahead!'

Nanny, who towered way above her companions, bent low. Seconds later the train plunged into the inky blackness of the tunnel.

''Elpppp!!' screamed Nanny, 'I 'ates the dark. It's 'orrible. Let me 'old your 'and, Duckyboos! I'm scared to blinkin' death! Let me hold your – '

But now they were out of the tunnel. Nanny sat back in her seat and breathed a sigh of relief. 'I 'opes there aren't any more tunnels. Aaargh!! Duckyboos, where are you?? 'E's *gone*, Mr Igor!'

Duckula's seat was now empty. Nanny stood up and flapped around. 'Pull the communication cord! 'E's varnished!'

'I can hardly imagine he's *varnished*, Nanny,' said Igor, relishing the thought of the trouble-free life he could lead if Duckula were immobilized like a statue in a thick coating of varnish.

'Well, *vanished*, then! 'E must 'ave fell out in the bloomin' tunnel!'

'Praise be. Peace at last!' murmured Igor, settling back in his seat and closing his eyes.

'So, Igor, you wouldn't even care if I *had* gone missing, eh?' came Duckula's voice from beneath his butler's seat.

'Just my little joke, milord,' said Igor, without even opening his eyes. 'I knew you were hiding under the seat; your beak was brushing against the back of my knees.'

'Hmmm! I hope so . . .' Duckula scrambled out and studied Igor's face for a sign of malice. 'Sometimes I'm not so sure about you.'

46

'Thank goodness you're all right, puddin'!' Nanny picked up Duckula and hugged him affectionately. 'You shouldn't play tricks like that on your ol' Nanny!'

'Put – *oof*! Put me – *oof*! Put me down!' Duckula struggled for breath. 'You're squeezing all the air out of – *oof*!'

Igor sensed that the train was slowing down. He opened his eyes and stood up. 'It seems we may finally have arrived at our destination, milord.'

'Yes, indeedy!' said Duckula excitedly. 'Will you kindly put me down, Nanny? We'll be getting off in a second!'

He broke free of Nanny's tender grip and strained to see what lay ahead in the darkness. 'I can see a platform!' he cried.

The train coasted along and came to a halt with a gentle squeal of brakes outside a deserted, tumble-down old station. Half of a broken sign on the booking-office wall read 'Pen' and on the floor was the other half, saying 'dingle'.

'Yippeee!' yelled Duckula, opening the carriage door and jumping out, followed by Igor, who alighted in a slow, stately fashion.

Duckula looked up and down the platform. It was silent, still and neglected, with no trace of a welcoming light anywhere.

'We'll ask the engine-driver the way to Hard Cheese Hotel,' suggested Duckula.

He and Igor walked along the length of the train, but as they reached the middle, a wheezy whistle

47

came from the engine, and it started to move forward.

'Blow!' said Duckula.

Butler and Count stood still, watching the carriages clatter past as they gathered speed. But as the last one passed they got a terrible shock: Nanny was still on board – sitting helplessly on her seat, with her legs dangling over the side of the carriage.

'Help, I'm stuck! I can't get out!' she screeched at the top of her voice.

Igor and Duckula ran alongside and each tugged at a leg, but to no avail; she was a creature of great substance – so great that a small crane or a fork-lift truck would have been required to pull her out of her predicament!

'You'll be okay, Nanny! Get off when you stop at a station and catch the train back. We'll wait for you at Hard Cheese Hotel!' shouted Duckula, as she sailed off into the night. 'Oh, and if you see a vending-machine, bring me back a couple of bars of milk chocolate!'

'How tedious!' declared Igor. 'I sincerely hope that she hasn't gone for good – oh, dear, that word *good* – ouch, I've said it again!'

'Don't worry, Igor – Nanny will be back with us again sooner than we think – sooner than we *want*!' quipped Duckula. He was trying to keep cheerful, but nevertheless he felt a chill of fear run down his spine as he stood in this bleak, lonely spot so far from home.

'What now, milord?' asked Igor.

'I think we should make tracks!'

'Make tracks, Sir? How can we do that? We don't have any rails or sleepers or spanners or – '

'Hey, *I* crack the jokes, Igor! I pay the wages, remember?'

'I think I remember,' murmured Igor, 'though it has been a while . . .'

'That will *do*, Igor! My, we *are* perking up now the sun's gone down and it's getting late! Now, what was I saying? Oh, yes. I was saying we should make tracks for the hotel. I see no point in lingering here any longer.'

'Even though the surroundings are so promising!' Igor's eyes shone brightly and he rubbed his hands in delight; it was clear that he thoroughly enjoyed the darkness and solitude of the place.

'Gee, I don't understand what makes you tick, Igor.'

'My heart, of course, Sir, plus one or two refine-ments I've had fitted over the years.'

'Yuck!' Duckula was repulsed by this remark. He moved towards the 'Way Out' sign that was swinging gently in the wind by a single screw. 'How you can revel in gloom and doom, I will never understand, Igor. Don't you ever long for a warm beddy and broccoli sandwiches and cocoa and model railways and radio-controlled aeroplanes?'

'Can't say I do, Sir. I wasn't made that way.'

Duckula considered asking Igor who *did* actually make him, but he was feeling the cold now. He pulled his cloak tighter. 'Here's the exit, Igor!'

A narrow, twisting path took them down to a dusty road. In the distance they could see lights, so they followed the road, hoping that it would lead to civilization – and Pendingle.

They were in luck! After only a few minutes of walking they arrived at a road-sign which read:

PENDINGLE-ON-SEA

Welcomes

Careful Drivers

'That's me – a careful engine-driver!' Duckula jumped up and down on the spot. 'Igor, go and knock at that house and ask the way to Hard Cheese Hotel!'

Igor followed his master's instructions and strode up to the front door of the first cottage in the village. He tapped the knocker lightly.

'Not today, thank you!' came a wavering, high-pitched voice from within.

Igor rapped a little more boldly.

'We already got double-glazin', thank you!' the voice wailed.

Igor tutted. 'It's just like the village back home,' he grumbled, banging really hard this time.

'An' we got central heatin'. . .an' a set o' them encycle – encycling – '

50

'Encyclopaedias!' boomed Igor in his deep, resonant voice.

It was obviously time to give up. He moved to the next cottage in the neat little terrace and tried his luck there.

'Coming!' This time it was the confident voice of a young woman. Igor cleared his throat, adjusted the knot in his tie and brushed back the sparse feathers on the top of his head.

The door was opened by the housewife, who took one look at Igor's gruesome features, screamed and slammed the door on his beak.

'You're useless!' laughed Duckula, joining Igor. 'Let a charming, debonair young bachelor try.'

'Do we have one, milord?' asked Igor sourly.

'I'll ignore that remark.' Duckula stepped up to the front door and knocked.

The door inched slowly open and the same young lady peeped out. Upon seeing Duckula she screamed even louder than before. 'Alf! There's a funny-looking duck with a black cloak on the doorstep!'

Duckula turned to look at Igor, who was stifling a snigger. 'You dare say a word, Igor, and there'll be a vacancy for a butler at the Castle!'

Suddenly the door of the cottage flew open! There stood an enormous man with a face like a punchbag and biceps bulging under his T-shirt. He was well over six feet tall – and his shoulders looked even wider. 'What're you two weirdies doin' scarin' my wife?' he boomed, making a grab at Duckula, who dodged nimbly out of the way.

'I'm sure you already have a set of our encyclopaedias! Sorry to bother you!' shouted Duckula, as he
and Igor sped down the road.

After ensuring that they weren't being followed,
the fleeing pair stopped under a street-lamp by the
village green to catch their breath. They didn't notice
an old tramp lying on a bench next to them.

''Ello there!' he said brightly.

Duckula and Igor, seized with panic, hugged each
other.

'Well, if it ain't a vampire an' 'is butler!' continued
the tramp. 'Straight out of Transylvania, no doubt.'

Duckula turned in surprise and saw the shabbily
dressed tramp. He relaxed a little. 'Why, yes, we
are, actually. Aren't you – afraid of us?'

'Not at all, pal, not at all! You live your life – and
I'll live mine. No problem,' said the tramp, waving
his arms about like a conductor at an orchestra.

Duckula warmed to him and slapped him on the
back. 'What a decent chap you are. If only everyone
were like you! Now, can you tell us the way to Hard
Cheese Hotel. I believe it's near here.'

''Ard Cheese!' said the tramp.

'Yes?'

''Ard Cheese!'

'Yes, Hard Cheese – but where is it?'

'I dunno. That's why I'm sayin' *'Ard Cheese* – 'cos
I don't know!' The tramp giggled inanely. 'I'm sorry,
friend – just my li'l joke. I always gets 'em wi' that
one. It's just round the next corner, you want. Look

out for the Tough Cookie Cafe, an The 'Ard Cheese is nex' door.'

'Sounds a most irresistible combination of food and accommodation!' observed Igor.

'Take care of yourself!' Duckula smiled at the tramp. 'You're a true gentleman of the road!'

Round the corner went Igor and Duckula. They spotted the Tough Cookie Cafe. In the window were posters, offering various tempting dishes at bargain prices.

'Boy, am *I* hungry!' Duckula licked his lips. 'I'll call in there tomorrow!'

But now the greedy young Count's appetite for food was temporarily forgotten, for there, next to the cafe and set back behind a small lawn was – Hard Cheese Hotel!

'Are we really here, Igor?' said Duckula, gazing at the once-impressive old building, which now, though welcoming, looked somewhat the worse for wear. 'Let's go inside and find this Horace Trumpetblower!'

Meanwhile, back at Hampton Court Maze, the two bats came out of the clock for a chat.

'Dmitri, do you have the time?' asked Sviatoslav.

'Certainly, Sviatoslav, it's – ' Dmitri stopped and smiled at his friend. 'Ha, ha! You nearly caught me with the old 'have you got the time?' joke . . . and the two of us living in a clock! Hee, hee! I've not heard that one since about 1152!'

'Over eight hundred years?!'

'No – I mean 11.52 this morning!'

The bats rolled about in a fit of laughter, but were brought back to their senses by a trembling in the Castle walls.

'Whoops!' said Dimitri, wiping his eyes. 'It must be dawn in Transylvania. The Castle's about to take off!'

'And without the duck and his staff!' giggled Sviatoslav. 'What a shame!'

'You know, I'm really scared of flying,' said Dimitri.

'No, you're not.'

'Yes, my friend, I'm scared.'

'No, you're not,' insisted Sviatoslav. 'You're not really scared of flying. *Crashing,* yes, flying – no!'

The bats fell about again, hooting with laughter.

Outside, a large group of people had gathered to wonder at the Castle which had arrived so mysteriously and without invitation in the centre of the Maze.

A young policeman was stepping up to the front door to investigate the strange presence of the Castle, when it suddenly gave an almighty shudder and began to vibrate alarmingly.

He ran back to the safety of the crowd and watched as the Castle became enveloped in flashes of coloured light and promptly disappeared before his very eyes.

'Well, I'll be blowed!' he gasped, taking out his little black book and pencil to make out a report. 'Wait till they hear about *this* back at the station!'

7

A Nasty Shock!

Igor held open the door of the Hard Cheese Hotel in order to allow Duckula to sweep in majestically. Instead, he tripped over the welcome-mat and fell flat on his beak.

The manager – tall, balding, tubby, and dressed in a gaudy big-check grey suit – was sitting at the reception desk. He burst out laughing at Duckula's plight, and then came waddling across, still smirking, like an overgrown budgie.

He helped Igor to lift the Count to his feet and then spoke. 'Hello there! Sorry about the mat – they're coming to nail it down tomorrow. That's not much consolation to you, though, I suppose. Now what can I do for you, Mr – '

'Duckula – Count Duckula!' said Duckula stuffily, straightening the ruffled feathers on his head. 'And this is my butler, Igor. I'd like to see Mr Horace Trumpetblower, if you please.'

Their host's eyes twinkled and he grinned. 'Oh, I get it – you two are the comedy act for tomorrow night's cabaret! I didn't expect you tonight, but I should have guessed when I saw your funny costumes! Your entrance was very spectacular, I must say!'

'Do you *mind*!' said Duckula. 'We've come all the way from Transylvania, and we're very tired!'

'Of course, of course!' laughed the manager, thinking that Duckula was joking. 'I'll show you to your room. But please tell me – which of you is Nitwit, and which is Nincompoop?'

'What?!'

'Don't tell me . . . you're Nitwit! The old chap looks just like a nincompoop!'

Duckula stamped his feet in annoyance. 'We are not Nitwit and Nincompoop! We are not a comedy duo! We have come to see Mr Horace Trumpetblower! Will you please tell him we're here!'

The grin left the manager's face, but his eyes were still smiling in disbelief. 'I'm sorry, but you can't see Horace.'

'Why not?'

'He's been dead for nearly ninety years!'

'Dead?'

'That's what I said! Uncle Horace passed away when Queen Victoria was on the throne. I'm his great-great-nephew, Jocelyn Trumpetblower.'

'Poppycock!' snapped Duckula, removing from his pocket a torn-out page from The Transylvanian Times. 'He put this advertisement in today's paper!'

For a moment Jocelyn Trumpetblower studied the advertisement that Duckula pushed under his nose, then he threw back his head and roared with laughter again.

'What's so funny now?' demanded Duckula indignantly.

'*You* are – Mr Nitwit! Where on earth did you manage to dig out this old newspaper from?'

'*Old* newspaper?' Duckula snatched it from Trumpetblower's hands and examined the date at the top. He fumed and turned to Igor. 'The first of October, *1888*! It's a hundred years old! Nanny's been reading one of those ancient papers she saves for a rainy day!'

Igor shuddered at the thought of the long, wasted journey, and wished that he were back in the dark and gloom of the Castle.

Trumpetblower nudged him with an elbow. 'Great gag, Mr Nincompoop! You'll be a riot at the show tomorrow.'

'Pardon me, but we shan't be appearing at any sort of function tomorrow,' said Igor firmly. 'We'll be going home.'

'After we catch up with Nanny,' Duckula reminded him.

Trumpetblower could now see that Igor was no comedian. 'Shame you've come all this way to buy an engine; there hasn't been one in these parts for the past twenty years . . .'

'Say, why does everyone keep saying there aren't any trains to Pendingle? We *came* on one!' cried Duckula.

'Now, now. You'll have me thinking you're Mr Nitwit again!'

'But it's absolutely true. I left my nanny on it!'

'Show me the tickets, then.'

'We didn't get any.'

'Funny train that doesn't give you tickets,' laughed Trumpetblower. 'You've had a hard day, young fellow. I suggest you and your butler stay the night here and get some rest.'

'Yes, we'll take you up on that offer, thank you,' said Duckula politely. To Igor he added, 'We'll stick around here to find Nanny.'

Trumpetblower ushered his two guests across to the desk and banged a big brass bell with his fist. *Ting!*

At the sound of the bell, double doors at the end of the hall were pushed open by a shambling stork-like old butler, who made his way slowly across to the desk.

'Wilfred, will you take our visitors to Room 5?' said Trumpetblower, passing the porter a key. He smiled at Duckula. 'It has a lovely sea-view, Mr – er – '

'Nitwit,' mumbled Duckula absent-mindedly, thinking fondly of Nanny – and cups of cocoa with chocolatey bits on top. 'I mean *Duckula!*'

'If you'll both go with Wilfred, he'll make you comfortable. Breakfast's eight till ten. I'll send up some bedtime drinks in a few moments. How does cocoa with chocolatey bits on top sound?'

'Like magic!' grinned Duckula.

'Boringly predictable,' murmured Igor to himself.

They plodded silently behind Wilfred up the narrow, winding staircase to the first floor.

'I heard what you said about comin' on a train,' said Wilfred suddenly in a doleful voice. 'An' I believe you!'

'Really?!' said Duckula. 'Why? Have you seen it?'

'Indeed I 'ave, Sir. Three or four times – an' always late at night, when most o' the village is in their beds!'

'Wow! Hear that, Igor?'

Igor nodded. 'Most interesting. Do go on, Mr Wilfred.'

'I reckons it's some sort of apparition – a *Ghost Train*!'

'Aw, you're kidding us, Wilfred. It seemed real enough to me when I was sitting on it. Anyway, I don't believe in ghosties!'

'There's others in the village who's seen it. They be afeared o' goin' near the track after dark. I think ol' Trumpetblower must've seen it too – but he'd never admit it. He'd be too worried about losing custom if there were talk of phantoms an' such . . .'

'You don't say!' exclaimed Duckula.

'I am afraid I *do* say!' said Wilfred sadly.

And thoughtfully (and a little fearfully) they all went to bed.

8

An Enemy on the Horizon

Duckula opened his eyes at ten o'clock the next morning. He blinked and looked around. Where was Nanny with his breakfast? Where was this strange place? Ah, yes, now he remembered.

A gentle snoring came from the next bed. He looked across and saw Igor snoozing gently with just his beak visible over the blankets.

'Fine butler *he* is! How humiliating for a count to have to wake up his own staff!' grumbled Duckula, throwing back the sheets and walking to the window with difficulty in the oversized pair of pyjamas loaned to him by Wilfred.

The glorious sunshine flooded into the pleasant little bedroom as he pulled back the curtain vigorously and looked outside. 'Phew! What a lovely place!' he cried out.

Hard Cheese Hotel could certainly boast an imposing view. Built near the edge of a high clifftop, it looked down onto a magnificent sheltered bay of huge craggy rocks surrounding the beautiful, sparkling blue sea that lapped on to an unspoiled sandy beach.

'Igor, wake up – we're going for a swim!' Duckula pulled back the sheets playfully, revealing the sleeping butler, dressed in a long, flowing nightgown.

'Yuck, what a sight you are, Igor! You look like a spook!'

Igor opened one eye cautiously and grimaced at the bright dazzling sunlight. He turned over to shield himself from it. 'Oh, how nauseating! What's happened to the darkness, milord?'

'Get out, you lazy lump! It's ten o'clock – we'll miss breakfast if you don't hurry.' Duckula threw off his pyjamas and splashed around in the washbasin.

Igor clambered out of bed slowly and deliberately, the same way he had done for the past few centuries. Then he strode regally over to the washbasin, rubbed his chin thoughtfully and filled the bowl carefully with a mixture of hot and cold water. 'Must get it just right – blood temperature, as always!' he mused.

'See you down in the dining-room, slowcoach! I'll save you some cornflakes!' shouted Duckula, now dressed. He left the room, slammed the door and skipped down the stairs.

In the entrance hall he encountered Jocelyn Trumpetblower, who greeted him warmly. 'Good night, Sir?'

'Good *morning*, you mean!' quipped Duckula.

Trumpetblower looked puzzled, then he saw the point of Duckula's useless joke and smiled weakly. 'Ah, yes – Mr Nitwit coming out again!'

'Any sign of Nanny? Did she turn up last night?'

'Afraid not, Sir. How will I recognize her, by the way?'

'Easy!' laughed Duckula. 'She's like nothing you've ever seen before, my Nanny. Big-hearted –

big *everything*. Just give me a shout if one of your guests has trouble getting through the door; that'll be her!'

Losing Nanny hadn't affected Duckula's appetite. After consuming the breakfast he was given, and then asking for seconds and thirds and fourths, he persuaded Igor to join him on the sands. Searching for Nanny was his excuse: a spot of sunbathing was the prime objective.

On the golden beach Duckula darted here and there, kicking up sand, digging holes furiously, rolling over and over and then collapsing breathlessly on his back.

Igor, perched on a towel, sat and watched the childish antics of his master. 'It was never like this in the *old* days,' he winced, knotting the corners of a handkerchief to form a sunhat, which he fitted carefully over his head.

Duckula stripped down to his shorts and ran into the sea. 'Look, Igor!' he yelled. 'I can see a little boat far out at sea!'

There was a small wooden fishing-boat out on the horizon; and Duckula would have been amazed if he'd known who was in it. It was none other than his arch-enemy, *Doctor Von Goosewing!*

'Ach, zees outboard motors, vhy do zey alvays go kaput when you need zem most!' cursed Von Goosewing, wrapping the starting-cord round the flywheel of the little engine for the hundredth time and pulling it in vain with all his might. 'Und zees unbearable clothes make things *zo* difficult!'

He pulled off his cunning disguise – a stiff oilskin coat and big floppy sou'wester hat – and flung them overboard in temper. Then he sat down heavily and sulked. He was exhausted with the effort of trying to start the outboard.

There wasn't a great deal of room for him, for the boat contained a contraption that resembled a huge washing machine. It was filled with dials and knobs, and had two thick wires which led to a large car battery. Pointing out to sea from the bow of the boat was a long, sinister-looking metal tube, like a gun barrel, with a telescopic sight mounted on top. It was obviously a weapon of great destructive power; well it was *supposed* to be, at least.

'I haff spent hunderts und thousands of marks und toiled night und day to perfect zee ultimate Wampire Waporiser; I haff a sitting duck – vell, a svimming duck, then – for a target; I haff zee battery fully charged and zee Waporiser fully primed; und vot happens? Zee liddle outboard motor packs in und spoils my plans! I haff my oars, ja, but by zee time I row into Pendingle Bay, you can bet your bottom dollar zat zee dreaded Count Dugula vill haff vamoosed! I really sink it's time I gave up zee life off a celebrated wampire-hunter und vent into teaching or became an estate agent instead!'

Von Goosewing jumped up and kicked the engine. *Phut, phut, phut!* It burst into life – and then promptly slipped off its bracket and fell into the sea with a satisfying plop!

'Milord, I must protest,' said Igor, holding a small plastic bucket in one hand, and a toy spade in the other. 'I simply don't have the commitment to build a replica of the Castle in sand. Please change your mind; show me some mercy, I implore you . . .'

'Well, I *suppose* we could forget it,' answered Duckula, lying stretched out in the sun. 'In fact, I've got a better idea now.'

'Better for *whom,* Sir – for me or for you?'

'For both of us. Look over there.' He pointed to long ledge which ran high up along the face of a cliff in the distance. 'There's an old railway signal up there. That must be the continuation of the railway line we travelled on last night.'

'Why, yes . . . I can see it, Sir. That must be where Nanny went. She may be up there somewhere at this very moment!' Igor sounded enthusiastic; anything, he thought, to divert Duckula's attention from the back-breaking task of building sandcastles.

'I'd like to go and see where it leads to . . .'

'A splendid idea, milord. A capital plan!'

'So I'll go and investigate while you stay here and build the sandcastle!' Duckula watched Igor's face crumple at his suggestion. Then he grinned. 'Only kidding, Igor – you can come with me!'

Climbing to the top of the cliff was not easy work in the warm sun. It was even harder for Igor, who complained that he was suffering from arthritis, lumbago and vertigo. But eventually they made it.

They peered down from their vantage point and could clearly see that the Pendingle line *did* run along the ledge that they had spotted from below. Duckula asked a passing tourist for the loan of his binoculars and scanned the track with them.

'Can you see anything of interest, Sir?' inquired Igor.

'No – just a few oddments scattered along the line – a travel guide to Great Britain . . . a tin of cocoa further along . . . and a crêpe bandage beyond that . . . then a teapot like Nanny uses . . .' Duckula stopped. 'Igor, they're all *Nanny's* things! She must have chucked them out of the train as she went along to leave a trail for us!'

He dropped the binoculars back into the baffled tourist's hands, thanked him and then pulled Igor along by his cuff. 'We've got to find her!'

They continued along the cliffs, looking over the edge every so often to keep sight of the track on the narrow ledge of rock below.

'It's like the scenic railway at a funfair,' said Duckula, glancing down for the umpteenth time. 'Hello, what's this? It disappears into a cave now!'

Igor took a look. 'Quite right, Sir. It goes into a sort of tunnel in the cliff face.'

'How on earth are we going to follow it now?' asked Duckula.

'We can't walk along the line; that's a terribly dangerous thing to do.'

'We could try shouting "Nanny", I suppose,' suggested Igor feebly.

'Tch! Always looking for the easy way out!' said Duckula rudely. 'Okay, we'll try it! NAN-NY! NAN-NY! WHERE ARE YOU?'

'NAN-NY! OH, NAN-NY!' joined in Igor.

Nothing happened, of course. Well, *something* happened: their shouts attracted a small, black poodle, which came running up and attacked Duckula's cloak. It sank its teeth into the material, hung on and tugged, growling.

'Another bright idea of yours, Igor!' said Duckula angrily, as he twirled round and round in an attempt to detach the dog, which was now also whirling round in the air, still hanging on to the cloak like an earring.

'Allow me,' said Igor. He went down on all fours like a dog and growled aggressively. 'Grrrrrr!'

The poodle, upon seeing this awful sight, shrieked and let go, then ran off, yelping, at full speed. It shot over the edge of the cliff a short distance away.

'Oh, no!' screamed Duckula. 'The poor thing's fallen over!'

He and Igor went to the spot where the dog had disappeared – and they made a remarkable discovery. The poodle, obviously a local character who knew its way around, was scampering down a long flight of steps cut into the rock, complete with a sturdy iron handrail. It lead downwards and then into a dark cave entrance on the cliff face. An old, broken sign that read 'Cliff Walk' lay on the top step.

'That's where we'll find Nanny, I'm sure of it. We'll go down there!' said Duckula triumphantly. 'After lunch, that is; I'm starving hungry!'

9
The Plot Thickens

Castle Duckula was now back at home. It had arrived back on its mountain-top in deepest Transylvania in its usual peasant-scattering style with terrifying tremblings, rumbustious rumblings and fearsome firework effects.

The place was deserted and deathly still, as if it were awaiting the return of its ghastly inhabitants. Nanny's pots and pans lay quiet and unwashed in the kitchen sink. Igor's metal polish stood in its cupboard, while the silverware on the table gathered dust and tarnished slowly. No birds sang, of course, in the Castle's grounds; they knew the place too well to come near. Only the tick-tock of the Castle Clock broke the eerie silence.

Sviatoslav the bat came out wearily on the hour and shouted to his buddy, 'Dimitri, my friend, come and talk to me!'

Dimitri appeared quickly and yawned. 'Nice to see you. I was falling alseep in there!'

'The place isn't the same when it's empty,' declared Sviatoslav. 'I miss 'em, you know. I miss the daft duck . . . I miss big fat Nanny with her screechy voice . . . I miss the ugly old butler . . .'

There was a long pause.

'Ask me how often I miss them,' continued Sviatoslav.

'Tell me, how often do you miss them?' said Dimitri obediently.

'Every time I pull the trigger!' screamed Sviatoslav.

The two bats spun round and wobbled with laughter so loud that it echoed down every passage and in every room of the deathly quiet Castle.

'Boy, they sure give you a lot of cheese in this place!' mumbled Duckula, cramming the last crumb of Stilton into his beak. He and Igor were finishing their lunch in the hotel.

'I think you'll find, Sir,' said Igor in his superior manner, 'that you are supposed to *choose* from the cheeseboard – and not, how can I put it – '

'Scoff?'

'Yes, precisely . . . and not *scoff* the lot.'

'I need my nourishment, Igor. I'm young – and alive!' laughed Duckula. He looked pointedly at his butler. 'Which is more than I can say for you with any degree of certainty.'

Igor ignored the insult; he was studying two characters who had entered the dining-room. One was tall with a lean, hungry look; the other, shorter and portly with a permanently bewildered expression.

'I say, milord, Jones and Dr Wotsit have just walked in!' murmured Igor in a low voice.

'Jones and Dr Wotsit? Who are *they*?' shouted Duckula. The new arrivals and all the other diners turned to stare at him. 'Oh, those coots we met at the Maze!'

Hemlock Jones and Dr Wotsit strode over to their table. 'Hello there!' said Wotsit. 'May we sit with you?'

'Be my guest!' Duckula waved his hand at the two empty chairs by his table. 'What an amazing coincidence that we should meet up again like this!'

'We shouldn't really be here,' explained Jones. 'Only when we got back to – to – er – '

'Baker Street,' said Wotsit helpfully.

'To Baker Street,' continued Jones, 'we found a note under the door – a desperate plea for help from Basketville Hall on Dartmoor. "Mortal danger surrounds us," it said. "Come at once!"'

'So we went,' added Wotsit, nodding vigorously.

'And what do you think?' explained Jones, banging his fist on the table and sending the salt and pepper pots flying. 'We couldn't get near the bally place! Whopping great hound prowling round the entrance, barking and growling. Took a piece out of Wotsit's cuff!'

Wotsit raised his wrist to display a ragged sleeve. 'Only house I've ever seen with a "Beware of the Dog" sign on the *inside* of the gate!'

'What did you do?' asked Duckula, wide-eyed.

'*Do*? Why, we left immediately, of course! Can't be doing with that sort of thing!' said Jones. 'Pity – it might have been a good case!'

'So why are you here?' said Duckula, nudging Igor, who was dropping to sleep after his midday meal.

'Well, we were so *near*! We couldn't miss a chance

of coming to Pendingle for a day or two. Such a lovely spot,' was Jones' reply. 'Wotsit and I have been here many times. We know it like the backs of our hands . . .'

'Really?! Then you can help us with a little mystery!' cried Duckula, sitting up. 'You'll have heard about the Ghost Train?'

'*Ghost train*?' Jones was puzzled. He glanced at Wotsit, who looked equally blank.

'On the old railway line,' said Duckula.

'*Railway line*?' Jones scratched his beak.

'Yes, it run along the cliffs by the beach,' prompted Duckula.

'*Cliffs*? *Beach*?' Jones chewed his fingers foolishly.

'Gee,' said Duckula sarcastically. 'I can see you're going to be *really* useful!'

'Steady on, old chap,' broke in Wotsit, defending his colleague. 'They don't call Jones the world's greatest detective for nothing, you know!'

'Oh, how much do they *charge*?' asked Duckula drily.

That evening Duckula, Igor, Jones and Wotsit sat in the hotel lounge along with Jocelyn Trumpetblower and a handful of other guests. They were watching Nitwit and Nincompoop, the comedy duo, doing their act.

Duckula was restless. He had wanted to go searching for Nanny in the afternoon, but Hemlock Jones had persuaded him to wait until nightfall; he was of

71

the opinion that adventures were more exciting and worked far better after dark. So the rest of the day had been spent listening to Dr Wotsit reading from a huge pile of tatty exercise books, in which he'd chronicled Jones' greatest cases. And, *boy*, were they chronic!

Nitwit and Nincompoop were chronic too. The audience were not responding at all to their corny jokes and knockabout act.

'Oh, dear, they're dreadful,' whispered Trumpetblower to Duckula. 'I don't suppose you and your butler would care to take over the stage?'

When the comedians started cracking duck jokes, Duckula decided it was time to go. He rose from his seat, and his three companions followed him across the room.

'Oh, look at *them*!' shouted Nitwit. 'Going to a fancy-dress party, boys? I didn't know it was Hallowe'en!'

'*No*!' yelled Nincompoop. 'They're with the Gravediggers' Convention. They're off to do a spot of overtime!'

Duckula, uncomfortably hot with embarrassment, gathered his band of fellow-investigators in the hall. 'Right, are we all ready?'

'Ready for bed?' yawned Jones. '*I* certainly am.'

'Me, too,' said Wotsit. 'I'm all in!'

'I mean are we ready to go out and find Nanny!' hissed Duckula in exasperation.

'*By George*, I remember now! Of course we're

ready. Wotsit and I will have the case wrapped up in no time!'

'Good. Now, what's our first move?'

Jones looked thoughtful for a moment and then spoke. 'No idea – give us a clue!'

'I thought we were going to explore the caves . . .'

'What? In the *dark*? Very dodgy! Should have gone this afternoon. Besides, we don't have a torch, do we, Wotsit?'

Wotsit shook his head.

'But you told us to *wait* until it was dark!' Duckula groaned. 'Never mind, I've got a better idea . . .'

The four of them trudged through Pendingle and along the path that led to the old railway station. Duckula's plan was to lie in wait on the platform for the Ghost Train, climb into a carriage when it stopped, and then see where the train took them.

They reached the station and sat together on a rotting bench outside the waiting-room. The night was warm and the sky cloudless. The moonlight gave Duckula and his team of sleuths a clear view of the station and its surroundings.

'Almost midnight,' said Duckula. 'The same time that we arrived in Pendingle last night. If the Ghost Train runs on time, it shouldn't be long before it's here!'

Hemlock Jones stood up to stretch his legs. Then from his inside pocket he produced a large magnifying-glass. He bent down quickly and stared through his glass at a brown patch on the floor of the platform.

73

'Found something, Jones?' asked Wotsit.

'Most definitely!' answered Jones.

Duckula's heart beat faster. 'What is it? A clue?'

'It's *mud*!' declared Jones triumphantly. 'A unique splat of mud – of a type which is to be found only in Cornwall!'

'But we *are* in Cornwall!' cried Duckula.

'*Are* we? Oh, yes. I remember now. Just goes to show how right I was!'

Wotsit patted Jones on the back and said to Duckula, 'Didn't I tell you he was the best?!'

There was no reply from Duckula, because his attention had been drawn to a gentle rumbling and clanking noise from down the line.

'What's that?' shouted the great detective, holding out his magnifying-glass at arm's length and peering through it into the distance. 'Elementary, my dear *bonehead*!' hissed Duckula. 'It's the Ghost Train. Sit tight – and be quiet, please!'

Chuff, chuff, chuff! Squeal! Squish! The old train pulled up at the station, just as it had done the night before.

Duckula, once again lost in admiration for the huge steaming monster, sat motionless and stared in wonder at it.

'Come on, milord,' said Igor gently, tapping him on the arm. 'We have a train to catch.'

The four crept across the platform, stumbled into the last carriage and took up their seats.

'*Ouch*!' complained Wotsit, squirming in discomfort. 'Don't they have any first-class compartments?'

The train jerked and started along the line in the direction of the beach. It rattled and shook and spat out soot; Duckula loved everything about it!

After a minute or so, the track started to climb. The old locomotive chugged hard to pull its load higher and higher until it levelled out on the narrow ledge which ran along the cliffs. The midnight view of Pendingle Bay, with the sea sparkling in the moonlight, was bewitching.

'Look, Igor!' cried Duckula. 'You can see the sands now!'

'Ah, yes,' agreed his butler, glancing across the bay with one eye, 'and it's far prettier by night than it was in that sickening sunshine this morning!'

The train roared on at a considerable pace until it was almost at the entrance to the strange tunnel in the cliff-face. Then it slowed a little and blew its throaty whistle as it plunged into total darkness. The noise of the engine was deafening now, and the tunnel filled with thick, white, damp steam.

'Intriguing!' yelled Jones.

'Totally uncivilized!' moaned Wotsit.

'Terrific!' shouted Duckula.

'Typical,' grunted Igor, folding his arms indignantly.

They were deep in the cliff and still in complete darkness, when the train suddenly came to an abrupt halt, throwing them forward violently. The tunnel was silent now, except for the low hissing of the stationary engine.

'What's happening *now*?' cried Duckula. 'Hey,

stop it! Which of you jokers is tugging at my cloak? *Ye-owww!'*

A big pair of hands, invisible in the darkness, grabbed him by the shoulders and pulled him over the side of the carriage.

'Help!' screamed Wotsit, as another pair of spectral hands removed him roughly from his seat.

Igor and Jones, protesting strongly, received the same unwelcome treatment, and within a matter of seconds the carriage was empty!

10
Taken Prisoner!

In Duckula and Igor's bedroom at the hotel, a chisel-blade appeared in the wall, making a small hole in the faded rose-patterned wallpaper.

The occupant of the adjoining room was none other than Doctor Von Goosewing, still intent on atomising Duckula with his latest vampire-vaporiser.

'Ha, ziss ist gut!' he croaked, tapping the sock-covered end of the chisel with a hefty hammer. 'Zanks to mine clever idea of putting a zock in it – I mean *on* it – I can chip avay wizzout vaking up zee dreaded Dugula. He'll be fast asleep in his liddle beddy by now!'

A complete brick came loose. Von Goosewing pulled it quietly from the wall and peeped cautiously through the hole. 'Himmel! I cannot see a sausage! Never mind, Dugula must be in there. Vhere else would he be at ziss time of night?'

The vampire-hunter turned to the huge piece of apparatus which stood by his side. Connected to it by a flexible hose, like a vacuum-cleaner's, was the shining metal tube with telescopic sight. Von Goosewing picked it up and pushed it through the wall into Duckula's room. Then he turned various knobs, flicked a number of switches and stood grinning. 'My dream hass come true. *Auf Wiedersehen*, you nasty old wampire!'

His finger reached out and pressed a large red button. Instantly the Vaporiser shook and danced like a badly loaded washing-machine. Then it blew what sounded like a loud raspberry, which quivered along the pipe and through the metal tube into the bedroom next door.

'*Yaaaaaaa!*' came a piercing cry.

'*Ja*, "yaaaaaa!" is just zee right word for it!' screamed Von Goosewing in excitement. 'Zat, my friend, is zee end of zee Dugula line!'

But then the bedroom door flew open and in marched the ragged, blackened figure of Wilfred the porter, thick smoke pouring from the smouldering tails of his jacket.

'Ach, *Dummkopf*!' exclaimed Von Goosewing irritably and without any pity. 'Who are you? Do you realize zat I haff jus' wasted all my wapourising power on you! Vot vere you doing in Dugula's room? I distinctly told zee hotel manager I vanted zee room next to zee liddle duck!'

Wilfred, who had popped into Duckula's room to ask him if he wanted cocoa, didn't speak – he growled. Then he took a step closer to Von Goosewing.

'Hey, no need to get nasty wizz me!' Von Goosewing jumped onto the bed and then off at the other side, to avoid the menacing advance of Wildred. Then he leaped across the room, out onto the landing, into Duckula's room and slammed the door shut.

Wilfred looked in amazement at the vaporiser and

went over to it. 'I wonder what would happen if I pressed this big red button?'

He pressed it.

'*Aaaaaaargh! Ye-owwwww!*' howled Von Goose-wing from next door, getting the full force of his machine's rays. '*Ouchhhh! Ow-eeeee!* A taste of mine own medicine is zee last zing I expected!'

Duckula, Igor, Hemlock Jones and Dr Wotsit were still in the dark – in more than one meaning of the word. They were sitting in a small, cold cave, into which their invisible assailants had thrown them. The cave was unusual in that it had a thick wooden door, which had been closed and firmly bolted behind them.

'I can smell baking. It's making me peckish!' said Duckula.

'So can I, milord,' agreed Igor, sniffing deliberately, as if he were trying to ascertain which particular item of food was in the oven. 'It's rather like Nanny's home cooking, don't you think? Only she tends to take it one stage further – to the point of incineration.'

Tears came into Duckula's eyes. He thought fondly of Nanny bending down at the stove in the Castle kitchen, removing her smoking, black scones and saying, 'I'll remember to turn the gas down a bit next time, Duckyboos'; but she never did remember, of course, and they always turned out like rock cakes.

He wiped his eyes on his sleeve and threw open a

question to the others: 'Any ideas what we're doing here, or who's taken us prisoner?'

'Not a clue, old chap,' said Jones.

'I never thought for one minute that you would,' retorted Duckula. '*Boy*, we're in a *real* fix now!'

'In a way, the darkness is rather refreshing, don't you think?' said Igor.

'For once I agree with you, Igor,' said Duckula. 'At least I don't have to sit and look at your face!'

Duckula waited for a response from Igor, but none came. So he stood up and felt his way round the walls, stumbling over his fellow captives.

'Ouch!' cried Wotsit. 'Who's got their foot on my hand?'

'Sorry, I'm sure!' Duckula was hungry and grumpy. 'But one of us has to make an effort to find a way out of this place! If only I could see . . .'

'Well, as I said before, I don't have a torch with me,' said Wotsit apologetically. He paused. 'Only matches and a candle, for emergencies. Jones and I have been in some really tight spots, y'know.'

'And what d'you think *this* is, if it's not an emergency – Igor's thousandth birthday party?' exclaimed Duckula. 'Get your candle out and light it!'

'If you insist,' murmured Wotsit in a huff.

After what seemed like an age of fumbling and scratching, a match flame flared brilliantly in the gloom, and Wotsit's wavering hand applied it to the candle, which then gave out a warm, friendly glow.

'Ah, now we can set about finding a way out of

here!' announced Duckula, surveying the walls of the cave. He went over to the door and tried it with his shoulder, but it didn't budge.

'This reminds me of a very similar situation in one of our lesser-known assignments, The Case of the Weedy Lumberjack,' murmured Wotsit. '*He* was stuck in a cave with a wooden door.'

'Tell us how he got out, then,' said Duckula impatiently.

'Easy as pie!' laughed Wotsit. 'Easy as pie!'

'Do you intend to tell us or not?'

'Oh, certainly, my dear fellow. He had a petrol-driven chainsaw with him. Started it up, cut himself a nice little round hole in the wood and then stepped out to freedom!'

'Well, thank you!' snapped Duckula. 'Thank you for that useful piece of information! Now, can we all *please* search for an escape route before the candle burns down?'

Wotsit stood in the centre of the cave, holding the candle aloft so that the others could examine the walls and floor for a hole of some sort.

Duckula came rapidly to the conclusion that the walls were solid. He looked up despairingly – and then spotted a narrow crevice in the roof! He pointed it out to the others. 'It's our only hope,' he said. 'Let's give it a try!'

'We'd never fit through there, milord,' said Igor.

'I know *you* wouldn't, Igor, and neither would the other two!' explained Duckula. 'But if *I* could get out, I'd fetch help! Now, stand under the hole – you, too, Jones. Wotsit, bend over, if you please!'

Duckula stepped on Wotsit's back and climbed on to Igor's shoulders. Jones steadied him by grasping his legs.

'Oooh! Hee, hee! Let go, Jones! You're tickling me!' giggled Duckula. 'Here we go – one, two, three – *hup*!'

He caught hold of the rough rock above, and launched himself into the hole. With a tremendous effort he crawled upwards until he could grip with his feet too. 'Boy, this is even harder work than Nanny's cycle exerciser!'

But Duckula was in luck! He found himself in a small natural passage which ran almost horizontally and made his journey much easier. It was still pitch black, and he wished he'd brought Wotsit's candle with him.

After crawling along on his hands and knees for a couple of hundred metres or so, he saw an encouraging glimmer of light ahead! He scampered along as fast as he could, and discovered that the passage terminated in a hole in the ground. Light flooded in from a chamber below, and Duckula could see that it wasn't a great distance to the floor.

He threw his legs over the side of the hole, lowered himself as far as possible without letting go – and then dropped the rest of the way.

'Gee! Where am I now?' he said out loud, to help overcome his feeling of fear.

The light was provided by an electric lamp hanging from the roof. Duckula glanced round and saw that he was standing not in a chamber, but in a much larger passage. There was a wooden sign on the wall, saying, 'This Way Round. Please Mind Your Head' followed by an arrow pointing in one direction.

'Ah, now I get it!' he cried. 'I must be in the Cave Walk. If I follow the arrows I'll come out on the clifftop!'

The arrows *did* lead Duckula to the clifftop. Five minutes later he was climbing the stone steps with the iron hand-rail, where that morning he and Igor had seen the black poodle.

At the top he sat and recovered his breath. His beak and hands were as black as the night sky, and his little cloak was torn and ragged. 'Nanny will go bananas when she sees it! Well, she would do, if she weren't bananas already!' he laughed with relief.

11

Wilfred Lends a Hand

Duckula ran from the cliffs into the centre of Pendingle village, looking for the police-station. He soon found it – a small cottage with a single blue lamp shining above the front door, and an old black bicycle standing beside it. All the windows were in darkness.

He pressed the bell repeatedly. At length a light came on in a bedroom and the window was flung open. The annoyed face of the bald-headed local bobby peeped over the window-sill. 'Yes?' he boomed. 'What is it?'

'Nanny's been kidnapped!' shouted Duckula.

'What?!'

'My Nanny – she's been kidnapped on the Ghost Train . . . I don't think it is ghostly really . . . and Igor, my butler . . . and two detectives from London . . .'

'Clear off, you young 'olidaymaker, and stop pesterin' me at this time o' the night!' shouted the policeman. 'Else I'll bring you in for questionin'!'

'It's *true*!' persisted Duckula. 'They're prisoners in a cave in the cliffs. You must help me to save them!'

'Take a word of advice, sunshine!' snapped the policeman, now poking his head right out of the window and revealing his pixie-patterned nightshirt.

'You go back 'ome an' stop messin' me about with your stupid stories. Ghost trains indeed – all a silly rumour!'

'But I live in Transylvania . . . and I can't go home without Nanny and Igor. Please come and do your duty!'

'Oi'll do my duty, all right! I'm comin' down an' chargin' you with disturbin' the peace. Wait there!' The policeman disappeared from view and slammed the window shut.

Duckula decided not to hang around; being arrested would not help his friends in the least. He walked off briskly in the direction of Hard Cheese Hotel with his head down.

'I'll help you to rescue them, Count Duckula,' a voice said brightly.

Duckula lifted his head and found Wilfred the porter was approaching him. 'Wilfred! What are you doing here?'

'You weren't in your room for bedtime cocoa, Sir. An' then I seen you runnin' past the 'otel like a bat out of a belfry.'

'It's very kind of you to look after my welfare, Wilfred, but I really don't know what you – '

'Believe me, I can 'elp you, Sir. You won't get nowhere with PC Bludgeon. 'E'll just put you in jail for the night – an' then where will you be?'

Duckula had no choice. 'Okay. What d'you suggest?'

'Let's try the ol' station. I could 'ave sworn I just

85

'eard that there Ghost Train clatterin' along the track!' said Wilfred.

'Did you?!' Duckula's eyes lit up. 'Right! The station it is!'

They moved silently and quickly through the deserted streets and headed out of the village. Dawn was breaking now: the sky was starting to get lighter and the early birds were waking up and trilling their morning songs.

As the pair neared the station, Duckula signalled Wilfred to walk quietly. They crept forward furtively round the side of the booking-office and peered round the corner at the platform.

The train was there, the engine hissing gently – almost as if it were waiting for Duckula and Wilfred.

'So *this* is the Ghost Train!' exclaimed Wilfred.

'What shall we do now?' whispered Duckula.

'Climb on board,' said Wilfred, 'an' go an' rescue your Nanny an' Igor!'

'Last time I went on it, I got dragged off in the dark and taken prisoner. I hope it doesn't happen again!'

'There's nothin' else we can do, Sir. We'll be all right – I've brought me trusty dinner-tray to ward off any attackers!' Wilfred partly removed a heavy and ornate silver tray from the inside of his jacket.

They stole across the platform and silently slipped into the rear carriage. At Duckula's suggestion, instead of sitting on the seats, they lay out of sight on the floor.

Duckula sniffed. He detected the strange baking

smell he'd noticed in the cave. Then he heard the engine give a chuff and felt the couplings take up the slack, jolting his carriage forward. He was off for his third ride on the mysterious Ghost Train!

The hidden passengers remained in their uncomfortable position as the train laboured up the incline and then increased speed on the level stretch along the cliff-face. It was light now. Duckula looked up at the clear blue sky and the cheering clouds of dense steam, and he dreaded the thought of going back into the darkness.

Moments later the train raced into the black tunnel. Further and further into the cliff it ran, and then it slowed down and stopped.

Duckula waited with his eyes closed tightly for the invisible hands to snatch him away; but they didn't. He opened his eyes, expecting to see nothing, but was amazed at what he *did* see!

The train had stopped in a gigantic underground cavern, brightly lit with powerful electric lamps that hung on long cables from the roof. The cavern was a hive of activity: against one wall was a long line of huge ovens pouring out heat; and the floorspace contained row upon row of tables littered with cooking implements and large baking-bowls. There were perhaps thirty or forty most unsavoury-looking cooks hard at work, rolling out pastry, cutting and shaping it and adding large spoonfuls of filling.

'Wow!' said Duckula, peering over the side of the carriage. 'An underground food factory! Doesn't it smell gorgeous?! Wonder if they give free samples?'

Suddenly Nanny came into view! She stumbled from behind the end of the line of ovens, pulling a great big truck piled high with trays of golden-brown Cornish pasties.

Duckula, overcome with emotion at seeing her again, almost shouted her name, but he stopped himself. 'Better get the others out first!'

He and Wilfred crawled out of the carriage and kept well out of sight by crouching down below some large packing-cases.

'I think,' said Duckula, eyeing a big, thick wooden door near the track a little way behind them, 'that Igor, Jones and Wotsit are in there. I can't be sure – it was dark when they put us in!'

'You go and investigate,' said Wilfred. 'I'll wait here and keep watch.'

Duckula, bent double, ran on tip-toe back along the line. The train provided perfect cover, and he reached the wooden door without being seen. He put his ear against it and listened.

'We'll have this case wrapped up in a jiffy!' he heard Jones saying. 'Brilliant idea of mine to send the young duck for assistance, Wotsit. You may as well start writing up an account of it all for your memoirs. I think we'll call it "Jones and the Curiously Incredible Case of the Ghost Train". Oh, and you may as well work out a fee for our services.'

'Huh! He's got a nerve!' said Duckula. 'He's a walking disaster! I've a good mind to leave him and Wotsit in the cave!'

He slid back the rusty old bolts as quietly as

possible and then pulled at the handle. It wouldn't move. He tugged harder until the door gave way a little with a loud squeak.

'What's that?' cried Wotsit.

'It'll be my rescue-party, of course!' announced Jones confidently, striding over to the door and giving it a mighty push.

The door swung wide open and took Duckula with it, squashing him almost flat against the cave's outside wall.

'How extraordinary!' exclaimed Jones. 'There's no-one here!'

Duckula wriggled out from behind the door and confronted Jones. 'What's the big idea of splattering me like that? I come to save you and this is how you repay me!'

'Sorry, my dear fellow! Just keen to get out of here; Wotsit's candle's nearly burned out.' Jones whipped out his magnifying-glass and stared at Duckula's apparel. 'I say, your clothes *are* in a mess! From the state of them, I deduce that you've – '

'That I've been crawling through tunnels on my hands and knees? I know, I know!' Duckula looked into the cave and saw Igor and Wotsit rising to their feet. 'Hurry, you two! We're getting out now!'

'Ha! Not so fast!' rasped a loud voice.

Duckula gulped and turned round to face a villainous figure, very short and extremely fat, dressed in a black suit and with the feathers on his head plastered down with hair-oil. He was accompanied by a bunch of heavies who were so ugly they made Igor look like a film-star.

But what astounded Duckula more than anything – and saddened him greatly – was the fact that Wilfred was with them, and obviously part of the gang!

'Allow me to introduce myself!' said the fat little man, grinning and displaying a mouthful of gold fillings. 'My name is Legs Sparrow. You may have heard of me!'

'Indeed I have, you bounder!' piped up Jones. He turned to Duckula and Igor. 'Why, he's the scourge of the East End!'

'The East End of London?' asked Igor, impressed.

'No – the East End of Pendingle, actually . . .' said Jones weakly.

'*Wilfred*! How could you lead me into a trap like this?' cried Duckula. 'I thought you were my friend!'

Wilfred, ashamed, spoke quietly. 'I'm Legs's look-out. I keeps an eye out for people who get too nosy about the train!'

'Bring the prisoners to my room,' snapped Legs. 'I suppose we'd better feed them while they're with us. I haven't quite decided what to do with them yet!'

Leg's henchmen pushed Duckula, Igor, Jones and Wotsit back along the side of the train. Legs led the group across the big cavern where the cooking operation was going on. The 'cooks' at their tables glanced evilly at the visitors as they passed by.

Duckula hoped to catch sight of Nanny, to let her know that he was safe; but there was no trace of her.

They were taken into a large makeshift office with filing cabinets, a desk, and a map of Europe pinned on the wall. Stuck all over the map were various coloured flags.

Legs sat in a luxurious executive chair behind the desk and then told the members of his gang to leave. 'Don't even think of escaping,' he said calmly to his captives. 'My colleagues will be on guard outside.'

'Don't think you can keep the world's most famous detective locked up like a caged animal!' burst out Wotsit.

'On the contrary, my dear fellow,' scoffed Jones. 'That's precisely what our Mr Sparrow is doing. But not for very long, I can assure him of that!'

'You mean you have a plan?' Duckula said softly out of the side of his mouth.

'Not an inkling of one!' whispered Jones. 'But it sounded good, didn't it?'

Duckula groaned – and then his tummy groaned. He was hungry again.

'Ah, breakfast's arrived!' Legs stood up and cleared a space on his desk to make room for a tray of hot food which Wilfred was carrying in.

'Let me guess what's on the menu,' said Duckula wistfully. 'Cornish pasties?'

12
Breakfast With Legs!

'On the contrary, my dear fellow,' said Legs Sparrow. 'It is not Cornish pasties!'

'Hey, you can't say that!' cried Duckula.

'Say what?'

'The old "on the contrary, my dear fellow" routine. Hemlock Jones says *that*; it's about the only thing he does. You're going to confuse the readers if you're not careful!'

'No, I'm not!'

'Yes, you are! Isn't he, Igor?'

'Indubitably, milord.'

'See!'

'Very well,' conceded Legs, laying the tray of food on his desk. 'Quite the opposite, then. In fact, it's cheese and pickle sandwiches for your breakfast – with a nice hot cuppa!'

'Oh, boy!' exclaimed Duckula. 'Tuck in, everyone!'

'No meat paste, I suppose?' queried Igor.

'Sorry,' said Legs. 'I'm a strict vegetarian. If I'd known you were coming, I'd have had a jar brought in specially.'

'You're a *vegetarian*!? So am *I*!' interrupted Duckula.

'How refined!' said Legs. 'I hardly ever come

across vegetarians; there don't seem to be many in my line of business – general racketeering and robbery.'

'Very cosy!' commented Jones icily. 'Watch him, Duckula – he's a silver-tongued fiend! One minute he'll be chatting like an old friend: the next minute he'll be setting your feet in concrete, ready for a swim in the river!'

But Duckula was no fool – well, not on this particular occasion, he wasn't. He winked slyly at Jones in an attempt to let him know that he, Duckula, was simply patronizing Legs: keeping him friendly until they could make some kind of escape.

Jones naturally didn't understand this subtlety. 'Something in your eye, Duckula?' he asked with concern.

'Mr Sparrow,' said Duckula, hastily changing the subject. 'If you're a criminal mastermind, how come you're running a bakery?'

'A good question – but it's top secret!' smiled Legs. He paused for a moment. 'Oh, go on, I'll tell you; I can't resist it!'

Duckula took the last two cheese and pickle sandwiches from the plate and gobbled them up.

'It's *because* I'm a criminal mastermind that I'm doing it,' continued Legs. 'In a nutshell, we're mass-producing sickeningly horrible Cornish pasties, filled with all sorts of nasty, putrid ingredients. Then we'll deliver them all over the country – that's why we have the train – *and* ship them to Europe as well.

The map, here on the wall, shows all our distribution points.'

'But why?!' cried Duckula. 'It's such a waste. You could make lovely vegetarian ones!'

'It's simple, if you think about it,' said Legs. 'Flooding the marketplace with grotty pasties that no-one can eat will cause an enormous demand for tasty ones. Everyone will be saying, "Dearie me, where can I get hold of yummy Cornish pasties the way they used to make them?" At that point I'll switch to making real ones again – to a vegetarian recipe, too, if you like. I'll back it with a big advertising campaign for "Sparrow's Wholesome Cornish Pasties" and clean up! It'll make me a millionaire overnight!'

'A brilliant idea!' enthused Duckula, secretly thinking that Legs must have lost his marbles long, long ago. 'Clever, eh, Igor!'

'Masterful, milord.'

'One last question, Mr Sparrow,' said Duckula, pouring out a cup of tea and shovelling in five spoonfuls of sugar. 'Why's Nanny working for you?'

'Nanny? Oh, you mean the big gal we found on the train? She's wonderful, and so strong! Y'know, she can carry two thousand pasties without any effort – with one arm, too; she seems to have the other one permanently in a sling!'

'Didn't she try to run away?'

'Dear me, no. She thinks she's working in a real bakery. Poor old thing's babbling on about saving up her wages to buy the train from me for some bimbo of a kid she evidently looks after!'

Duckula felt a surge of anger at the exploitation of his dear Nanny, but he controlled himself. 'Ha! Would you believe it!' he laughed.

'And, listen to *this*,' giggled Legs. 'I've seen her eating some of the pasties – and *enjoying* them!'

He finished his tea and put his cup down. 'I must get on with my work now.'

'Yes, you must.' Duckula rose from his seat and signalled his companions to do the same. 'We'll be off now, Mr Sparrow. Nice to meet you. Don't worry about your little secret – we won't breathe a word to anyone. I'll collect Nanny and we'll see ourselves out . . .'

'You'll be *off*?!' The affable expression left Leg's face. His eyes narrowed and he twisted his beak into an ugly snarl. 'Do you seriously think I'm going to let you all walk out of here just like that?!'

'Told you he was a nasty piece of work,' said Jones smugly.

'You're always right, Jones, always spot-on!' added Wotsit loyally.

Legs gave a sharp, piercing whistle that brought his gang of thugs running to his side. 'Lock Robin Hood here and his Merry Men back in their little nest for a spell. I need time to decide their fate . . .'

It was another sunny day in the outside world: children splashed about on the sea-shore; grannies sat and knitted in deckchairs; and couples strolled aimlessly along the beach.

In a secluded bay not too far away, however, was

a most peculiar sight! A partly inflated airship was drifting a couple of metres in the air, tethered by two ropes fastened to strong wooden stakes hammered into the wet sand.

Doctor Von Goosewing was there too, surrounded by the paraphernalia of his vampire-vaporiser. But, instead of lying back and soaking up the warm summer sunshine, he was hard at work – trying to complete the inflation of his airship with a small cylinder of gas.

'Ach, ziss liddle boddle of gas I borrowed from zee balloon lady at zee sweetie-shop is zimply not enough for mine beautiful Zeppelin Mark 3. Vhy do I haff to sink of everything? Vhy iss everyone except me zo useless? You'd expect somebody to haff a drop of helium gas wizz them . . . but no, it's "try zee sweetie shop on zee promenade" and when you schlepp all zee way there, it's a case of "I've only got a titchy bit left till zee delivery-man comes tomorrow"!'

A small child licking an ice-cream cone wandered up to the airship and poked at it with his finger. 'What you doin', mister?'

'Vot does it look like I'm doing, liddle boy? Haven't you ever zeen a Zeppelin before?'

'No!'

'Ach, children today! No interest in zee finer zings in life! Ziss iss a Mark 3 Super Deluxe – zee luxury ship of zee air. Take a peep through zee cabin vindow, liddle buddy, and you'll see zat it has everything you could possibly vont: a cocktail cabinet wizz lashings of lemonade; a microwave oven; a colour television; a reclining armchair; and a radio alarm clock!'

The youngster stood on tip-toe and peered into the cabin. 'No direction-finder?' he asked.

'Vell, no – not yet.'

'No radar?'

'No, actually.'

'No altimeter?'

'Er – I haff ordered one . . .'

'No back-up system if your engine fails?'

'I'm afraid not!'

'You wouldn't catch me going up in that! What happened to the Mark 1 and the Mark 2?'

Von Goosewing went red in the face. 'Zee Mark 1 and Mark 2 you say?'

'Yes, that's what I said.'

'They – er – crashed a liddle bit . . .'

'Proves my point exactly,' said the boy, biting off the bottom of his cornet and sucking the ice-cream through. 'You want to get some better equipment fitted in this one!'

'Ach! Zee cheek of it! Telling me to get better equipment, when you see before you zee very latest in wampire-waporisers! Kindly go and take a running jump – preferably off zee end of zee pier!'

'Get lost yourself!' retorted the child, giving the flabby airship a kick. 'Stick a pin in it!'

Von Goosewing put down the gas cylinder he was holding and chased the child away. 'Clear off, you pest, and don't come near me again!'

The hot sun was drying out the sand quickly, making it soft once again; and the wooden stakes holding the mooring-ropes had been working loose. Now a breeze blew across the beach, caught hold of the airship, which tugged at its ropes, and yanked the stakes clean out of the ground.

Von Goosewing, still shaking his fists at his fast-disappearing young technical adviser, turned to see his beloved Zeppelin drifting silently away.

'Stop!' he yelled, running after it and struggling to catch one of the trailing ropes. 'I command you to stop at vonce, you stupid great balloon!'

He managed to grab hold of a rope and hung on to it, but it didn't do him any good. It simply lifted him into the air too – and took him, dangling and screaming, out to sea . . .

Duckula and his friends were back to square one again. They sat miserably in the cave, with a dim, flickering light their only comfort. Legs had grudgingly given them the privilege of a small lantern.

'We're really in a fix this time,' said Duckula, looking up at the roof. 'They've done a good cement job on my secret passage!'

'Did I ever tell you how we escaped from the bank-vault in the strange case of The Crooked Counterfeiter?' asked Wotsit.

'Don't bother,' replied Duckula. 'I suppose you had an oxyacetylene cutting torch with you!'

'Why, yes – you're right!' marvelled Wotsit. 'Some

workman had left one in a corner over the weekend. However did you guess?'

'Elementary, my dear birdbrain,' said Duckula. 'You couldn't find your way out of a shower cubicle without the wonders of science at your disposal!'

'All in all, this has proved to be a most disappointing trip, milord,' announced Igor spontaneously. 'No locomotive for sale . . . Nanny kidnapped . . . incarceration in this cell. I'll be glad to get back to the Castle.'

'Do you really think we'll ever see the Castle again, Igor? Do you think we'll ever taste Nanny's cooking anymore?'

'Of course we will, Sir. The Duckulas have always been a resourceful bunch. There was that sticky spell during the medieval times, of course. The peasants were very clued-up on witch-hunting and vampire-clobbering and burning at the stake . . . but we pulled through all right. Things are much easier nowadays.'

'You know, Igor, when we get back – *if* we get back – I'm never, ever going to complain about Nanny, or poke fun at you or play practical jokes . . .'

'Thank you, Sir,' said Igor. Then he added quietly, 'A likely story!'

'Shhh!' hissed Jones. 'Listen! There's someone behind the door!'

Someone was slowly sliding back one of the bolts. There was a short pause and then they heard the other one being opened.

'Maybe it's Nanny!' whispered Duckula, holding his breath.

The door opened slowly – and Wilfred crept in!

'Huh!' said Duckula. 'Have you come to gloat at us, you traitor?'

'No,' answered the subdued Wilfred. 'I'm letting you out. I can't let Mr Sparrow keep you locked up like this; you're my friends.'

'Oh, Wilfred! Thank you!' Duckula put his hand on the porter's shoulder. 'I knew you weren't really a criminal!'

'Let's go,' said Wilfred gratefully, 'before I'm missed!'

He checked that the coast was clear, then ushered the band of prisoners out of their cave. He pointed down the tunnel. 'Follow the track and you'll come out on the cliffs in Pendingle Bay.'

'What if we get squashed by the train?' shivered Jones.

'You'll be quite safe,' said Wilfred. 'They daren't use the engine durin' the day or they'd be seen.'

'We can't go without Nanny!' exclaimed Duckula.

'Tut! I forgot about 'er!' Wilfred scratched the top of his head. 'Wait here an' I'll fetch 'er.'

Duckula peeped round the locomotive and watched Wilfred go to the far end of the huge cavern. He saw him walk casually up to Nanny and whisper to her; and then he saw her drop an armful of Cornish pasties in surprise. *Clang*!

'My Duckyboos over *there* by the train?!' she

screamed at the top of her voice. 'I must go an' see 'im at once!' Then she charged across the cavern at full speed, banging into tables and knocking pasties here, there and everywhere.

Her screeching alerted Legs and his gang, who came running to see what was the matter!

13

Nanny Gets Fired

'You know, Dimitri, the duck and his cronies must be having a whale of a time in England,' said Sviatoslav.

'Without a doubt, my friend, without a doubt!' replied Dimitri. 'There's nothing more refreshing than a good holiday. Tell me, are you going anywhere this year?'

'Nothing planned; I'll probably stay at home and do some jobs around the Clock,' grinned Sviatoslav. 'Anyway, I'm still sore from skiing last year.'

'Yes, I remember now, Sviatoslav. You broke your leg in three places, didn't you?'

'That's right, Dimitri. I broke it in Austria, Switzerland and the Transylvanian Alps!'

The two bats creased up in peals of laughter.

It was no holiday for Duckula and company; no picnic either – Duckula hadn't eaten for, well, minutes!

Nanny picked him up and squeezed him, like a boa constrictor crushing its prey. 'Oooh, me little darlin'! Nanny's missed you somethin' terrible!' she cried. She saw Igor, Jones and Wotsit standing close by. ''Ello, Mr Igor! You 'ere too – with your friends from the Maze?'

'Unfortunately, yes, Nanny. Have they treated you well?'

'Wonderful, Mr Igor; an' the food's marvellous! Lovely 'ot Cornish pasties to eat whenever you want! An' best of all, Mr Sparrow – 'im what runs the place – 'as promised to sell me this 'ere steam-engine if I does a few days' work for 'im! That means the young Master will 'ave two!'

'How very kind of Mr Sparrow,' said Igor cynically, touched by Nanny's innocence.

'Me Duckyboos is very quiet, aren't you? Is there somethin' wrong? You tell me if there is!'

Duckula, still in Nanny's vice-like grip, moved his beak but nothing came out. He squirmed and kicked his legs and tried to prise himself out of her arms.

'Oh, 'eck! No wonder 'e's gone quiet! I'm cuddlin' 'im too 'ard!' Nanny let go. Duckula, gasping, dropped like a stone to the floor. She picked him up and sat him on her arm like a ventriloquist's dummy. 'Speak to me, dumplin'!'

'Phew, that was close, Nanny! I feel like the end of a toothpaste-tube. You've got to learn to control those biceps! Good to see you, though!'

'How delightful to see such a happy reunion!' said Legs Sparrow, who, with his unattractive comrades, had circled round them. 'Nanny, would you mind returning to your duties, please? There's a truck full of pasties that need taking down to the jetty, where the boat's waiting. Your friends and I have a little business to sort out!'

'Right you are, boss!' she shrilled cheerfully, snatching a Cornish pastie off one of the trays on the train and offering it to Duckula.

'I don't eat meat, Nanny – remember?'

'Ooh, so long as you're not off your food. I'll 'ave to keep a watch on you!'

'Yes, please do that, Nanny!' said Duckula. He realized that he would shortly be locked up again, and it was comforting to know that Nanny would not be far away; there was a chance at least that she could free them.

So he was upset and angry when Igor suddenly shouted, 'Nanny! Mr Sparrow is nothing but a wicked crook! He's going to lock us up, and he'll probably try to feed us to the fishes. Don't do any more work for him – and don't eat any more of those pasties, whatever you do!'

Nanny stared at Igor as if he were raving, and then turned to Duckula. 'Is 'e off 'is trolley or is 'e tellin' the truth, Duckyboos?'

'It's all true,' said Duckula sadly.

'Right, then, Mr Sparrow, this is the last Cornish pastie I'm movin' for you!' Nanny raised the pastie she was holding and squashed it on Legs's head.

'Why, you – ' Legs took a step towards Nanny, but Duckula jumped in front of her.

'You touch one feather on Nanny's head and you'll have me to answer to!' he snarled. Igor was surprised; he'd never seen Duckula so angry.

'Ha!' said Legs with a slight tremble in his voice.

'I – I wouldn't waste my energy. Lock 'em all up, boys, and Wilfred too!'

'Don't put Nanny in with us, I beg of you, Mr Sparrow,' pleaded Igor. 'She'll drive us mad with her non-stop chattering!'

'Good! I hope she does!' snapped Legs. 'Boys – make sure you put her in the cave with the rest of 'em . . .'

'Igor, what's got into you?' demanded Duckula, as they were all led away. 'Why did you have to get Nanny locked up? Now we've got as much hope of escaping as a stick-insect has of tripping up an elephant!'

'Trust me, milord, just trust me,' was Igor's enigmatic reply.

If, reader, you'd been in Pendingle Bay on that bright, warm day and glanced upwards, you might have seen high in the blue midday sky far above the clifftops a curious, slow-moving, silvery cigar-shaped blob.

You might have run around in panic shouting, 'UFO! UFO! We're being invaded!' But if you'd put a coin in the telescope on the cliffs and focused it carefully, you would have instantly identified the blob as a Zeppelin Mark 3 airship. You wouldn't? Tut, tut! Recommended reading for you is 'The Illustrated Airship Spotter's Guide' by Goosewing, Doctor Von, and published by Klatter and Bang, price 25 Transylvanian drachmas – or swop for good three-speed bike with no spokes missing.

Let's join the author of the book right now, as he sails through the heavens over the Cornish coastline . . .

'Achtung, you wiscious wampire, your days are numbered! In fact, your minutes are numbered! Mine deadly accurate wampireometer tells me zat you are somevhere down there in zee cliff caves, Dugula, and zee instant you step out of zem – kaput! – I mean kerpowww! – you vill be – er – kaput!'

Von Goosewing leaned precariously over the side of the little observation platform at the back of his cabin, scouring the landscape for a sign of Duckula. The whole airship tilted dangerously. Goosewing dashed back to the centre of the cabin to regain the stability of his craft.

A shortage of helium gas was Von Goosewing's problem; and it was only thanks to a last-minute delivery of balloon gas to the resort's sweetie-shop that the intrepid sky-pilot was airborne at all.

'Ja, ve're ready and waiting for you ziss time, Dugula, you slippery demon of darkness!' he cackled maniacally, fondly stroking the huge humming vampire-vaporiser that almost filled the cabin. 'Your end is near! Ha, ha, ha! Hee, hee . . .!'

Duckula, Igor, Jones, Wotsit, and now Nanny and Wilfred, too, sat in a cheerless circle in Legs's cave cell.

Duckula was fed up; not merely because he was spending his third term of imprisonment there, or due to the cramped conditions, but mainly because

106

rescue seemed so remote, now that no-one in the outside world knew where they were. He had no idea that Doctor Von Goosewing was hovering far above, waiting to zap him into oblivion.

'Want to play ludo, Duckyboos?' said Nanny, producing a complete board game from her sling. She then brought out a handful of other games. 'Or snakes and ladders? Or draughts? What about a lovely game of bingo, then?'

'Not in the mood, thanks, Nanny.'

'Suit yourself! 'Ow about you, Mr Jones? Or you, Dr Wotsit? No? Oh, by the way, don't go without takin' a look at me corns, will you?'

'Er – perhaps we could wait till – um – we have a little more light!' Wotsit floundered for an excuse to avoid conducting the most revolting examination in the whole of his medical career. 'Oh, and I've retired from practice, by the way; I'm very rusty.'

Nanny fumbled in her sling again and pulled out a boiled sweet. The others watched hungrily as she popped it in her beak and crunched it. 'Sorry, it was me last one!'

'You wouldn't have a chainsaw in there – or an oxyacetylene torch, I take it?' asked Duckula.

'No, you know your Nanny don't carry dangerous things that her little Duckyboos could 'urt 'imself with. Matches and blowtorches is not allowed!'

'Nanny doesn't need such things,' said Igor quietly, half-opening one eye at Duckula and then closing it again.

'What?' Duckula barely heard him.

'Think about it, milord. When Nanny wants to reach the other side of a door, what does she do? Does she turn the door-handle gently and then walk calmly through?'

'I wish she did!' smiled Duckula. 'We'd save a small fortune in repairs. Hey . . . Igor, I see what you mean! If she smashes through all the doors at home, she can just as easily walk through this one!'

'Precisely, Sir! Now do you appreciate my reasons for getting Mr Legs to imprison her along with the rest of us? It was a cunning ploy!'

'Brilliant, Igor. Remind me to give you a wage increase!'

'All right, milord – give me a wage increase!' Igor's shoulders shook, as he chuckled deeply at his little joke.

'Legs go, then!' said Duckula, standing up. 'Get it, Igor? *Legs* go! Oh, never mind!'

'With respect, sir, I think we should wait for our opportunity. I'm sure that those so-called cooks out there must be due for their lunchbreak soon. I think that would be the best time for – er – *Operation Nanny*.'

'I'll start explaining the plan to Nanny right now,' said Duckula. 'That'll give it time to sink in!'

14

A Chase Through the Tunnel

Igor was right! Wilfred confirmed that production of the tainted food would stop for an hour at one o'clock. The prisoners waited patiently until they heard a long, loud whistle being blown in the cavern.

'There we are!' said Wilfred. 'Now, give all the workers time to put down their pastry-cutters and walk to the canteen nearby. . . . I think we should be all right about – now!'

Duckula helped Nanny to her feet and pointed her at the door. 'Okay, Nanny, go through it like you always do!'

Nanny marched up to the door and banged straight into it. *Bam!* The door shuddered and shook, but remained closed! Nanny backed up a few steps and tried again. *Bam! Thud!* Still the door stayed resolutely shut. A third attempt was also unsuccessful.

'That'll do, Nanny!' cried Duckula. 'The door is as tough as old boots. Wonder who made it? We could do with him at the Castle!'

'I believe that Nanny could do it with a few more lunges,' observed Igor, 'but I'm afraid that the noise would bring Legs and his gang.'

'You're right,' said Duckula dejectedly. 'Oh, why can't someone just slide back the bolts and let us out? I'd reward them with a timeshare holiday at the Castle.'

As if in answer to his plea, the bolts on the door were drawn back! Duckula jumped in surprise.

'Drat!' said Jones. 'They must have heard us!'

The door opened fractionally and a small beak poked through the gap. 'Na-nny, are you-a in there?!'

The voice was familiar to Duckula and Igor, but they couldn't quite place it. Nanny, however, recognized it immediately and pushed the door open wide. 'Toni!' she cried.

Their saviour was none other than Toni, the waiter she'd met on the train from London!

He stepped into the cave with a smile. 'Hello there, everyone!' He beamed and then looked lovingly up into Nanny's eyes. 'You're-a safe now, my leetle chicken. Toni has come to take you away from-a here!'

'Oo-er!' said Nanny, shyly. 'What are you doin' here?'

'Is a long story,' began Toni.

'Make it short then, please!' implored Duckula.

'Well, you only meet a girl like Nanny once in your-a life . . .'

You can say *that* again, thought Duckula.

'. . . and when I see her-a going down the platform at Penzance, I say to myself, Toni, you must forget your-a coffee cups and your-a sandwiches and go after her. So I did! The ticket-collector tell me that

110

you all-a set off walking for Pendingle – and I follow you!'

'It was *you* who was running after us on the Ghost Train?' asked Duckula.

'Yes, it was. But my leetle legs were not quick enough. So I have to walk to Pendingle!'

'But how did you get in *here*?'

'By accident! I walk for miles in the dark. On and on, through a leetle station with no name – '

'Ah, yes,' said Igor. 'I remember the sign was broken. It was difficult to spot.'

'Evidently I walk-a too far. I go through the spooky tunnel in the cliffs and finds myself in this-a place. I see these men questioning Nanny, and I say to myself, Toni, she's in big trouble. So I hide in a packing-case, waiting for my chance to rescue her!'

'You've been here all this time?' gasped Wotsit.

'That's right! When I hear the lunchtime whistle blowing, I climb out to find Nanny, and then I hear the loud banging on your-a door – and here I am!'

'Are we glad you *are*!' exclaimed Duckula.

'Yes, it's lovely to see you again, Toni!' squawked Nanny. She pulled a scrap of paper from her sling. 'I kept your phone number, see!'

Toni rolled his eyes in delight. 'And I thought you'd have forgotten all about me by now!'

Igor, who hadn't much time for this sentimental talk, said, 'Don't you think we should be going now, milord?'

'Quite,' said Duckula. 'Now, what shall we do?'

111

'I have an ingenious escape plan!' cried Jones, waving his hands in the air.

'Keep it for your next adventure,' said Duckula wryly. 'I have a much better one. I haven't thought of it yet – but I guarantee it'll be better than yours!'

'You know,' said Toni, 'working for the railways has taught me one thing: how to drive an engine! Shall we go out in style?'

'Brilliant!' Duckula understood immediately what Toni was suggesting. 'Will you sneak out and get into the cab of the loco? Then we'll all follow and jump into one of the carriages?'

'Consider it done. Give me one minute. *Ciao* for now!' Toni slipped through the door and disappeared from sight.

'Hope he's not a double-agent!' said Jones.

'Good thinking!' said Wotsit. 'Perhaps we'd all better stay here in case it's a trap!'

Duckula sighed and wondered if Jones and Wotsit had ever even solved a crossword-puzzle. He checked his watch and waited until a minute had elapsed. 'Okay, everyone, let's go!'

They all crept stealthily out of the cave – Jones and Wotsit, too; in truth, Nanny couldn't claim to be stealthy, but she did her best.

Duckula opened the door of the rear carriage to allow the others to file in silently. Then he climbed aboard and helped Nanny to scramble over the side. She landed awkwardly and almost crushed Wotsit.

'Helppp!' he yelled.

'Shhh!' hissed Duckula.

Toni, leaning over the side of his cab saw that everyone was safely on board. He rubbed his hands in glee and faced the vast array of levers, copper pipes, dials and big brass knobs. Then his face dropped. '*Mama mia*!' All these controls! They're not a bit like-a the diesel engines!'

He checked there was still a good fire burning, shovelled on a couple of extra scoops of coal, and then picked a small important-looking lever at random. 'This must be the one!' he cried, closing his eyes and pulling it.

Chuff . . . chuff . . . chuff, chuff, chuff! The old engine spurted out steam and started moving – but forwards, instead of backwards!

'Whoops-a-daisy! Wrong direction! I should have pushed the bambino lever, not pulled it!' He tried to move it the other way, but it was stuck fast! He tugged hard, but it was useless!

The train continued along the track, which ran to the end of the cavern. It ploughed into tables, breaking them up and knocking pastry and ingredients to the floor. It also caught the side of Leg's little wooden-built office and brought it crashing to the ground. Legs was inside, talking on the telephone to an influential underworld contact. He screamed in terror as pieces of timber and plasterboard tumbled onto his head.

The train crunched against the rock wall of the cavern and stopped, still belching out thick steam, which added to the confusion – and provided an excellent smoke screen!

113

'Quick!' yelled Toni. 'Make a run for it!'

His passengers didn't need telling. They jumped out of the carriage, pulled Nanny over the side and raced down the track towards the tunnel, with Toni chasing after them.

Legs shouted for help. The members of his gang came running out of the canteen. Two of them began pulling at the wreckage of his office to release him; and the rest of them plunged into the fog of steam, slipping and sliding on the carrots, potatoes and pastry that covered the floor of the cavern.

Through the black tunnel fled the escapees, feeling the side wall for guidance. Faster and faster they ran, as they gained confidence, until they saw an arch of daylight in front of them.

'Nearly there!' spluttered Duckula. 'Everyone still together?'

'Yes!' chorused six voices.

Chuff, chuff, chuff! Legs's boys had managed to put the train into reverse and had started down the tunnel, too!

'Hurry up!' shouted Duckula, panicking at the sound of the engine. 'The train's coming! We're going to get caught on the narrow ledge along the cliff!'

A very familiar airship was hovering low over the track where it left the tunnel. Doctor Von Goosewing, clutching the barrel of his vampire vaporiser, was leaning dangerously over the side of his observation platform and keeping a lookout.

'Hee, hee, hee!' he chuckled. 'Mine wampireo-

114

meter reliably informs me zat Dugula is on zee move. According to zee dial, he is due to come out of zee mouth of ziss tunnel at any moment . . . and then it's vindow-blinds – I mean *curtains* – for zee liddle fellow!'

Duckula and Nanny were the first two to tear out of the tunnel, closely followed by Jones and Wilfred and Toni. Igor and Wotsit, chugging wheezily along behind, their arms going like pistons, looked like miniature versions of the steam-engine that was pursuing them.

The first thing Duckula saw was a long rope dangling in front of him from the sky. His eyes followed it upwards, and he saw that it was a mooring-rope trailing from the airship above. He had a sudden brainwave! 'Grab hold of that, Nanny!'

Nanny, mystified, did as he said.

'Now climb up it!' he panted. 'Quickly!'

She shinned clumsily up the rope, and Duckula held the end for the others. 'Everyone up the rope!' he urged. 'It's our only chance!'

You may remember that Von Goosewing's airship was delicately balanced. Nanny's bulk alone would have been enough to upset it badly, but the weight of the seven desperate individuals, hanging onto the rope for dear life, tilted the Zeppelin through a ninety-degree turn, making it point upwards like a skyrocket.

'Himmel! Who are zese dratted creatures getting a free ride on the end of my – *yeowwww*!' Von Goosewing fell forward as the airship swung to a vertical position, and he tumbled straight out! '*Helppppp*!'

He fell through the warm blue sky onto the beach below and landed with a plop on a beautiful sandcastle which had just been completed by the small child he had met earlier; the one whom he had chased away for making derogatory remarks about the airship.

The sandcastle was a total write-off, and, in temper, the child bashed Von Goosewing repeatedly over the head with his toy spade.

'Leave me alone!' screamed the Doctor. 'Stop it at vonce, you liddle horror or I'll – I'll set zee wampires on you . . .'

Meanwhile the Ghost Train – not in the least ghostly in daylight – hurtled out of the tunnel. Legs, at the controls, saw Duckula and his friends hanging from the airship. He jammed on the brake and watched helplessly as his enemies drifted serenely away to safety.

One by one, Igor, Wotsit, Wilfred, Toni, Jones and Nanny dropped from the rope onto the soft, golden sands. Only Duckula remained; he'd spotted a fast motor-cruiser moored at the end of the bay, where the cliffs met the sea – and it had given him another brainwave!

He climbed up the rope and struggled into the airship, which now resumed its normal horizontal attitude. Squeezing past the deadly vampire-vaporiser and wondering what on earth it was, he reached the controls of the Zeppelin Mark 3. 'Oh, boy,' he grinned. 'Am *I* going to have fun!'

Duckula switched on the engine that drove the thrust propellor, and then grabbed the steering joystick. He guided the airship down and across to the boat he'd seen in the water. Then by careful manipulation he managed to make the airship hover in a stationary position right above it.

A quick glance confirmed his suspicion that the boat was the one Legs used to smuggle his gruesome grub across the sea: it was laden with small crates of pasties.

'Ahoy there!' he shouted to one of Legs's ruffians who was sitting at the wheel. 'Tie me up, will you? I'm drifting!'

The scallywag looked up and smiled, thinking that the airship was out of control and that Duckula was surrendering. He reached for the dangling rope and secured it firmly to a cleat on his boat. 'Okay, duck! come on down – I'm ready for you!' he growled menacingly.

'And I'm ready for you!' laughed Duckula, pushing the speed controller. The engine roared and the airship rose high into the air, lifting the dangling boat and gangster clean out of the water. The sea was awash with pasties!

'Hope the fish have the good sense to leave 'em alone!' giggled Duckula.

He turned the airship back into the bay until it was over the clifftops, and carefully lowered the boat onto the railway line on the ledge by the tunnel. Then he picked up a sharp knife and sawed through the rope, leaving the stricken cruiser well and truly high and dry!

15

Homeward Bound

That evening, the dining-room of Hard Cheese Hotel saw great celebrations!

Around a large table sat Duckula, Nanny, Igor, Jones, Dr Wotsit, Toni – and Wilfred, who had been forgiven. The remains of a large feast lay on the table, and Duckula was even too full to scoff all the cheese.

'What an adventure we all 'ad!' sighed Nanny.

'I'll say!' said Jones.

'I'd very much like to add it to our collection of "Curious Cases of The World's Most Famous Detective",' mumbled Wotsit.

'I'm sure you *will* do!' giggled Duckula. 'Can I take it you won't be charging us a fee for your vital part in the day's events?'

Jones pursed his lips and consulted Wotsit. 'What d'you think, Doctor?'

'Just our expenses will suffice,' he said with a serious expression on his face. Then he burst out laughing, and Jones joined in.

Duckula put his arm round Nanny. Well, as far round as he could manage – which really wasn't very far at all. 'I'm going to take better care of you in future, Nanny.'

'Oh, get away with you, silly! It's me that's goin'

to take care of you – for ever an' ever!' Nanny elbowed him with her sling arm and knocked him clean off his chair. She hastily picked him up again and re-seated him like a rag-doll. ''Ere, I've got somethin' for you. I got it special this afternoon.'

'Not a pastie, I hope,' said Duckula, watching Nanny fishing around in her sling.

Eventually she produced a gift-wrapped box and passed it to him. Eagerly he tore away the paper and found – a brand-new model railway!

'It's to replace the one I trod on, Duckyboos.'

'Aw, you shouldn't have spent your money on me!' Duckula dabbed his damp eyes with his napkin.

Wilfred and Toni looked tearful too. They sat in silence.

'You two have very long faces,' said Igor, bringing them into the conversation. 'Nothing wrong with long faces, of course; I'm quite partial to them. But is there something the matter?'

Wilfred answered first. 'I feel so terrible about what I did to you all; you're so nice. I should never 'ave done it. I couldn't resist the money that Mr Sparrow offered me, you see. It was just plain greed.'

'No problem! I asked Mr Trumpetblower to give you a raise – and he agreed!' said Duckula. 'So forget it, and do cheer up!'

Wilfred was relieved at hearing these comforting words. He smiled at Toni.

'And may I ask what's eating *you*, Toni?' continued Duckula, 'although I think I know already.'

120

"E's upset about me, Duckyboos.' Nanny amazed Duckula by speaking in a low, tender voice; he'd never heard her utter a word in anything less ear-splitting than a squawk. "E asked me to stay 'ere in England with 'im instead o' goin' back to the Castle.'

'I ask her to *marry* me, actually,' said Toni.

The room fell silent.

"An I had to tell 'im no.' Nanny's voice wavered. 'My place is back 'ome with me Duckyboos . . .'

There was another long pause.

'You can stay if you want, Nanny, you know that,' said Duckula.

Nanny looked at him but she didn't know what to say.

'She too fond of you, Count Duckula!' laughed Toni bravely. 'You are-a the luckiest person I ever 'ave known. You 'ave your Castle an' your wealth – but most of all, you 'ave your lovely Nanny!'

Jones broke the silence. 'What will you do now, Toni? Go back to London?'

'I – I don't think so,' answered Toni. 'Paddington station will 'old such memories for me. I think I will take a little break. I will visit my mama who lives in the North.'

'Ah, Northern Italy – beautiful!' purred Igor.

'No, North of England,' said Toni. 'Chorlton-cum-Hardy is the place I call home.'

'The name rings a bell,' said Duckula thoughtfully.

'Never heard of it!' murmured Wotsit. 'Sounds like a fairy-tale setting.'

121

'In a way, it is,' replied Toni dreamily. 'I think so, anyway.'

The dining-room door burst open and in strode Jocelyn Trumpetblower. 'Hello, everyone!'

Jones nodded a greeting. 'Any news of Legs Sparrow and those other rapscallions?'

'Oh, no trace at all,' said Trumpetblower. 'I went and told PC Bludgeon the whole story, but by the time he'd pumped up his bicycle tyres and pedalled to the cliff, they were all long gone! The only things left were the Ghost Train, a boat on the tracks and about a quarter of a million in used pasties!'

'So! Legs Sparrow remains free to fight another day!' yelled Jones, dramatically thumping the table. 'Oh, sorry – didn't mean to make you all jump!'

Trumpetblower had more to say. 'I also did a little research into the Ghost Train. Turns out it *was* the one that Uncle Horace owned.'

'So he never did sell it . . .' said Duckula to himself.

'Apparently it crashed and lay unwanted in the tunnel on the cliffs. Legs Sparrow must have restored it to its former glory in order to start the Ghost Train legend to keep people away at night,' went on Trumpetblower. 'If you're willing to accept it, Count Duckula, I'd like to present you with it as a gift!'

Duckula stood up, overcome by his host's generosity. 'Thank you – but no thank you,' he said slowly. He tapped the model railway that Nanny had given him. 'This will suit me fine. *You* must have the Ghost Train, Mr Trumpetblower; it'll be a great attraction for your hotel!'

He sat down again.

'Why did you refuse the train, Duckyboos?' asked Nanny in bewilderment.

'Because, Nanny,' said Duckula with a gleam in his eyes, 'I'm now into *airships*!'

For all we know, Doctor Von Goosewing is still wondering what happened to his Zeppelin Mark 3 Super DeLuxe airship.

Serves him right, the silly old sausage, that he doesn't know it arrived very late one night at a certain Castle on a certain mountain-top in Transylvania and scared the village peasants half to death.

No, he never saw three dark figures – one of them very loud and very squawky, one duck-shaped, and the other a round-shouldered butler-type – slide down the mooring rope, tie it to the knocker of the big front door, get the key from under the mat and go into the Castle.

'Hey, Dmitri, I got some news for you.'

'News, Sviatoslav? What news?'

'They're back!'

'You're kidding, my friend!'

'No, it's true. I just saw the demented duck running down the corridor with goggles and a flying helmet on!'

'A corridor with goggles and a flying helmet on?

123

Now I know you're joking! Hee, hee, hee!'

'Ha, ha, ha! Ho, ho, ho!'

That's all for now, reader. I hope you enjoyed the story. If you've ever wondered why there isn't a railway track spiralling up the mountain to Castle Duckula, well now you know!

Don't forget to look out for a low-flying Duckula in an airship when you draw the curtains at bedtime tonight. Wave to him, if you like; he'll be glad to see you – especially if you have any broccoli in the fridge!

Enjoy your cocoa. Goodnight and sweet dreams – *whatever* you are!